Between
Water
and the
Night Sky

First published 2023 by
FREMANTLE PRESS

Fremantle Press Inc. trading as Fremantle Press
25 Quarry Street, Fremantle WA 6160
(PO Box 158, North Fremantle WA 6159)
fremantlepress.com.au

Cover design Nada Backovic, nadabackovic.com.
Cover images 'Chinese Canopy with Dragon Among Flowers in the late 1100s', The Cleveland Museum of Art, rawpixel.com; Natural History Canary, thegraphicsfairy.com.
Printed and bound in Australia by McPherson's Printing, Victoria, Australia.

A catalogue record for this book is available from the National Library of Australia

9781760991845 (paperback)
9781760991852 (ebook)

Department of
Local Government, Sport
and Cultural Industries
GOVERNMENT OF WESTERN AUSTRALIA

lotterywest
supported

Fremantle Press is supported by the State Government through the Department of Local Government, Sport and Cultural Industries.

FSC
www.fsc.org
MIX
Paper from responsible sources
FSC® C001695

Fremantle Press respectfully acknowledges the Wadjak people of the Noongar nation as the traditional owners and custodians of the land where we work in Walyalap.

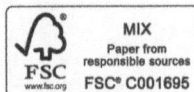

Between
Water
and the
Night Sky

SIMONE LAZAROO

FREMANTLE PRESS

In memory of Judith,
and for anyone trying to bring light and
meaning to incomprehensible darkness.

Simone Lazaroo was born in Singapore and migrated to Australia as a child. She wrote novels and short stories before completing her PhD in 2004 and teaching creative writing for several years at Murdoch University, where she is now an honorary research fellow. She mentors emerging writers and is in a Spanish-funded research group, writing about aspects of migrant experience, cosmopolitanism and cross-culturality.

Her five previous novels, and short stories, have been published in Australia, Spain, England, USA, Portugal and Cuba. Several of her novels have won or been shortlisted for Australian and international awards. Her novel *The Australian Fiancé* is optioned for film and she is currently writing two new works, one set in a coastal community in Western Australia and the other in Mediterranean Europe. She is a regular ocean swimmer, walker and unofficial rubbish collector at her local beach near Fremantle, Western Australia.

Contents

My mother told me photography means 'writing with light'. That my father's lost ephemeris divided twilight precisely into three phases. So I wonder, as the sun sets over the Indian Ocean, when do the golden minutes pass into the blue?

The Dark Room

NIGHT SHIFTING

MY mother's hand is still warm in mine. In the silence after she turns to face the darkness and exhales one last time, her eyes stay open but do not blink. I'm surprised by the low howl of some lost creature rising from me.

Past, present and future collapse. Tenses collide. She was my mother? She is my mother? She will always be my mother?

My only mother.

The nurse hurries in. She must've heard my cry. She checks for my mother's pulse, looks at the time. 4.05 a.m. Nothing but darkness outside.

'She's gone, love,' the nurse says apologetically, retreating to the doorway with her observation file. Keeping a respectful distance.

My mother's hand cools only slightly as the moments pass. I don't let go of it. Then I notice her chest rising and falling, almost imperceptibly.

'She's still ... breathing!' On the threshold of hope once more.

The nurse glances at her, steps forward to check my mother's pale wrist again, shakes her head sympathetically. 'It's not uncommon to imagine that. She's definitely gone. Sorry.' The nurse pats my shoulder, sidles through the door. Clears away a couple of empty bottles from last night's happy hour.

My mother's foundations were never strong, but she kept a roof over our heads for as long as she could. Now her place in time is collapsing, her life a house of unlucky cards; nothing beyond but darkness and a place we've never been together or seen. Now it seems only this cold fall will last forever. Shivering, I'm glad I changed her into her warm nightdress and socks before the ward lights were dimmed all those hours ago.

Her eyes gazing towards the dark sky look even larger than they were before, but what's almost unbearable is their expression of both resolve and fear, like that of some small nocturnal creature searching for scarce food in an immense night. Faith was always such a struggle for her: faith in any god, in other people, but most of all, in herself. She had her reasons for this, reasons that were too traumatic to reveal to anyone else. Except me, in her final years, when some memories weighed too heavily on her. Too much for an old woman to carry alone. I helped carry them, carry them still.

Outside, the sun dipped into the river and the crickets sang the night in. That was how my mother had begun telling me about her life. But near the end, sometimes blood came from her mouth instead of words. The stains on her shawl and pillowslip, like the imprint of a rose pressed too hard.

How long had I been in that peculiar state of shock called grief? Hours? Days? Months? Ever since her diagnosis. As I'm wishing that I'd thought to take one last photo of her before she died, the night-shift nurse returns with another nurse and clears her throat.

'Do you have a funeral company in mind?'

'No.' Not ready. Never will be. I wanted my mother to live forever.

'We'll need to contact one soon. There's nowhere to ... keep her here. We'll phone one for you. Any preferences?'

'She wanted cremation.'

'Sure. An all-woman team? Eco-friendly?'

'She'd like both. But not the ones who wear the silly hats. She'd want it simple and inexpensive.'

'Sure. Why don't you go and have a cup of tea while we wash her?' the nurse suggests. It sounds almost like our past week's morning schedule here. But it's clear the bigger plan for my mother was wrong all along. The doctors told us her disease would progress quite slowly, over months, at least until the end, but it's gone too fast all the way. Death has not waited long enough.

I walk down the palliative ward corridor. In the rooms either side, those alive are still sleeping under white cotton blankets, cocooned against the worst. Outside the window of the visitors' room, the first birds are calling too early before the first light; the first rain of autumn is falling too soon. The teabag makes the water from the urn smell like old vase water, the room looks desolate, despite so many flowers. All those bouquets given and abandoned by the loved ones of the dead.

The nurse calls me back. They've changed my mother into her thin white summer nightdress, laid her on her back with her arms by her sides and firmly rolled a white towel under her chin. Her nightdress's Bon Nuit label is just visible at her thin neck. Her expression and position are fixed, her skin paler. I cover her shoulders with the faded magenta silk shawl from Singapore's Little India all those decades ago when my father's love for her was strong; I take her hand. As if this will help me hold onto the life that's already left her.

The nurse pauses at the door again, offers me some transparent blue plastic bags labelled:

PATIENT'S NAME. PATIENT'S ADDRESS.

As if my mother still had another life and place to go besides death.

'Take whatever of hers you wish to keep. We'll … manage the rest.'

The nurse leaves me to do the leaving by myself. Hospitals' hospitality only stretches so far; another hard lesson I've learned since she was first diagnosed. They always need more beds, especially on this ward.

Pack into my mother's small shabby Great Wall suitcase her velvet slippers, dressing-gown and messages from all the people who loved her but couldn't make it across vast distances or misunderstandings to visit. Lift the silk shawl from her shoulders. Because she's worn it most winters since we migrated across the Indian Ocean to this cooler climate and the thought of it turning to ashes with her is unbearable. Because nothing can stop her body growing cold now. And because I still can't let go of her completely, though I've been rehearsing for years. Hold her hand and kiss her forehead beneath her wispy silver hair one last time, her belongings too light in my other hand.

It was like this on my first day of school: case in one hand, my other hand refusing to let hers go when the bell rang. Only a few months later, she tried to leave home, weeping, lugging a suitcase into the early morning. I'd run after her.

'Not far to go,' she said when I persuaded her to return home. Mother, how many times I tried to coax you back across the frightening distance of your sadness, back to your precarious home.

But not this time. I hope she saw more than darkness in her final moments. I wonder fleetingly if she would want a paper True Body from the funeral accessory makers in Singapore, to carry her from death to somewhere more eternal. But is there anything more eternal than death?

Now the pale sun rises between clouds dimmed by drizzle; the river carries the first glimmers of a new day towards the ocean. Infinity. I wish she could've seen that view as she waited to die.

Her nocturnal eyes, set on a future she will not live, remain open. Her cheek is cold when I kiss her one last time. The kitchen staff downstairs start clanging kettles and saucepans, making breakfast. The nurses are handing over. The night shift is ending. The day-shift nurse is at the door.

Time to leave my mother. To begin the longest shift. My feet step through the palliative ward doorways towards the hospital exit, marking the beginning of life without her. But the thresholds between my past, present and future seem to have vanished altogether. Only a glimpse of the Indian Ocean carrying the night over the horizon and beyond. Ocean without end. She was, she is, she will always be my mother. How far I would go to bring her back.

Meeting of
Two Worlds

SONGS OF LOVE AND WARNING

FRANCIS Oliveira disembarked at Fremantle Harbour from the P&O ship *Carthage*, anxiously showed his passport and answered the sunburnt Australian Department of Immigration officer's numerous questions. He lugged his Great Wall of China brand cardboard suitcase to a taxi, gave the terse driver the address of the student boarding house in West Perth.

Cicadas sporadically farewelled the day as the taxi crawled along the highway, growing shriller as he alit outside the boarding house. Not as loud as the evening crickets back home, though. And the plants in the front yard much sparser and more grey than green, barely a garden at all.

Dragging his suitcase up the cracked concrete path and over the verandah boards, he knocked on the boarding house's flyscreen door, peered into the dim hallway. No-one to greet him. He longed for a plateful of his sister's Devil Curry, but the hallway smelled of boiled potatoes and burnt milk. Not even the faintest hint of spice. The landlady had left his room key in a crumpled envelope scrawled with *Mister Oliver Vera* stuck on the door of the locked reception office. The first of many mistranslations he would endure in Australia.

❋

He almost collides with a pale, full-cheeked young woman as he carries his suitcase down the hallway.

'Sorry lah,' he murmurs, his hand dark against her pale forearm. The shock of their difference on that February evening in 1959, years before Perth's first Chinese restaurant opened its doors nearby, and the White Australia Policy was finally abolished. Such restrictions, despite the Indian Ocean lapping the shoreline only a few miles away.

'No need to apologise.' She smiles tentatively but warmly at him, as if she would like to say something more, before hurrying away through the front door.

Outside, the sun dips into the river and a lone cricket begins singing the night in.

❋

The next morning, Francis notices the young woman emerge from the room directly opposite his. Despite this proximity, they seem latitudes apart. Through her doorway, he glimpses brightly coloured clothes draped over every surface and erupting from three leather suitcases, as she quickly pats the loose bun of chestnut hair at her nape and pulls the door closed behind her. He has already unpacked his suitcase and put his clothes away. They fill only half the narrow oak wardrobe.

In the small dining room with its mismatched wooden chairs and laminex table, they exchange names and discuss the day's weather over a breakfast of toasted stale white bread and Bushells tea stewed in an aluminium teapot. His body is compact, slim, economical. She crosses her forearms over her plump belly.

Finishing his last corner of toast, Francis asks Elspeth Green to walk with him to the river across the road from the university. He brushes the crumbs fastidiously from his Robinson's department store Chinese New Year sale trousers as he rises.

'Okay.' Her smile, shy but warm, shows no teeth but makes her flushed cheeks even fuller. 'Where're you from?'

'Singapore. That island below the Malay Peninsula? Like the dot below an exclamation mark, lah. My parents are from Kuala Lumpur and Malacca.'

'What're you studying here?'

'Engineering, specialising in water supply. I'm on a Colombo Plan Scholarship. Singapore needs expertise to develop new pipelines and deliver unprecedented convenience and hygiene,' he explains. 'You can't have a clean new city without sewers.'

She smiles. 'Sounds like poetry.'

'Just commonsense,' he says proudly. 'And what are you studying?'

'Arts. Literature and French. Tell me about your life in Singapore?' Her voice rises tentatively at the end of every question, as if she is unsure of herself.

He tells her in a rush as they walk to the river.

※

He comes from one of Singapore and Malaya's ethnic minorities, the Kristang Eurasians, of Portuguese and Asian ancestry. When he was eleven, the Japanese invaders imprisoned his father, an immigration and customs officer, for allegedly helping the British destroy Singapore's main harbour so it would be useless to the Japanese. They banished the rest of his family and their church congregation to eke out an existence in the Malayan jungle. Like his family, many of the congregation were Kristang people. In the jungle they ate mostly yams, the only food they could easily grow there. They saw old and young friends die there from starvation and illness; he nearly died of malaria.

He hadn't aspired to saintliness as his mother had hoped when she named him Francis Xavier, but after they returned from Malaya to Singapore, he was swimming champion of his Catholic boys high school. He had taken up swimming to build his muscles, depleted by wartime malnutrition, and developed an interest in swimming pools, reservoirs and other bodies of water as he looked for places to train. He fortified himself with Milo and Dutch Maid powdered milk after double helpings of kuey teow from Singapore's street hawkers. When he had spare pocket money, he bought himself a small serve of Singapore Cold Storage's ice-cream.

⁂

He doesn't mention to Elspeth the other unnameable appetites he has felt since then. But he confides that he already misses Singapore's food.

'It's much spicier and tastier lah.'

'I would like to try that one day.'

In front of them, the river widens and carries reflections of the bright blue sky. They sit tentatively on a green park bench, careful not to get too close to each other.

'Where does this river go?'

'To the Indian Ocean.'

'I just crossed that ocean. Thought it would take forever.' He closes his eyes momentarily to try to forget the seasickness and the Fremantle immigration officer's prolonged questioning of him on arrival. 'And you? Are your parents Australian?'

'My father came from England in his early teens.'

'I am a British subject too,' Francis says, pulling with a flourish from his wallet the carbon copy of his Australian Immigration Department's REGISTRATION OF ALIENS form and pointing to one of its typed lines and the officer's scrawled answer:

NATIONALITY: *British subject.*

But he tries to conceal with his other hand the following lines:

WHETHER PREDOMINANTLY OF EUROPEAN RACE AND APPEARANCE:
No. Predominantly Asian.

Stuffing the form hastily back into his trouser pocket, he observes, 'Such a wide river. What's it called?'

'The Swan River. Named after the black swans found here.'

'Black swans! I thought all swans were white.'

'A lot of things here are not as you'd expect. The local beer is called Swan Lager. It has a black swan on its label. The brewery's just upriver from here.'

'Ah. But this river is much cleaner than the Singapore River. We should swim in it.'

'I've never really learned to swim,' she confesses. 'But I can float and tread water.'

'I can teach you. Swimming makes you feel free and strong. Like you can go on forever.'

※

When my father-to-be and mother-to-be caught the train one afternoon to the beach just north of the harbour where he'd disembarked from the ship weeks before, she would only paddle, lifting her cotton dress slightly above her knees.

'My skin burns too easily on days like today,' she explained.

He stared at her pale pink knees and calves, much broader and apparently softer-skinned than his and his family's back home. Elspeth was so unlike them all in so many ways that Francis felt both fascinated and slightly anxious around her.

'I swim,' he said, diving in just beyond the break-line. But as he turned his head each time to breathe, he felt reassured by her watching over him in the unfamiliar waters.

※

Arcs of tiny quicksilver fish breached the sea's surface between them once, twice, three times. Glad the waves weren't too big, Elspeth watched Francis's lean limbs cut through the deepening water as precisely as blades. Would she ever tell him about her recurrent nightmare of trying to call for help as an enormous, furious wave overwhelmed her in an ocean so deep no trace of her would ever be found again?

The sun's white glare in her eyes now, making it impossible to see Francis clearly as he swam too far away.

※

During their next walk along the river foreshore, Francis tells Elspeth proudly that he is a member of Singapore's Photography Club and its classical music appreciation club, but left his photographs and his Mozart, Chopin and Beethoven records behind because of luggage restrictions.

'I brought my camera though. It's a Box Brownie,' he says proudly.

Elspeth knows very little about cameras. 'Can it photograph far away things?' she asks lamely.

'All the way to infinity if you focus the lens the correct way, lah.'

'But you can't see infinity, can you?'

'Not exactly.'

'It's one of those things you have to imagine?'

He looks uncomfortable at that question, so she continues quickly, 'Tell me more about Singaporean food.'

'Ice-cream is my number one favourite,' he enthuses. 'Even though many British expatriates have gone back to England, now the Chinese are copying English ice-cream.'

'You can get lots of ice-cream here. *Peters. The health food of a nation*,' she intones. 'Isn't there anything more … exotic you eat in Singapore?'

'Exotic to you maybe. Singapore's people and food come from all over Asia. My favourites are longevity noodles and short soup from China. Jelabi sweets and crispy poppadums from India. From Malaysia, roti chanai and nasi lemak.'

'What's nasi lemak?'

'A plate of fried rice, crispy fried peanuts and whitebait, and a small serve of curry. Usually chicken. The gravy turns the rice golden and tastes of spices and coconut.' He looks longingly across the water to the far side, his thick-framed glasses reflecting the river darkly, concealing his eyes from her. She feels weak with hunger despite the toast in her belly; wonders if she had bigger appetites than most of the young women around, and not only for food.

'Your face looks red,' he observes.

'The weather.'

'The heat here is dryer than Singapore's.'

'Let's get our feet wet.'

Oblivious to two young women scrutinising her disapprovingly from the park bench, she kicks her sandals off. He places his new Bata sandals carefully next to hers, rolls up his new trousers fastidiously above his knees. Paddling in the shallows of Matilda Bay, she blushes when he points out her feet are as large as his.

*

At dinner a few evenings later, Elspeth and Francis had fish and chips from the kiosk near Matilda Bay. He was careful to eat the last chip and fragment of fish, but threw the crumbs on the ground for the seagulls.

'So you belong to a classical music appreciation club in Singapore.'

'Yes.'

'What's your favourite classical music?'

'Mozart, Beethoven. Chopin too.' He mispronounced Chopin.

'I like *Chopin*'s nocturnes. I like most classical music,' she smiled. She looked downriver, hoping she hadn't embarrassed him by correcting his pronunciation. 'Tell me about … is there any traditional … K-kristang music?'

'Oh, they're just kind of like folksongs, in a sixteenth century Portuguese dialect.' He shrugged dismissively. 'Songs of love and warning, that kind of thing, lah.'

'All in the same song?' She saw the half-moon reflected in his spectacles.

He frowned slightly. 'Sometimes yes, sometimes no.'

The warm evening had swallowed the weak sea breeze. She dabbed surreptitiously at her forehead.

'Let's test the water,' he suggested, kicking off his sandals.

As they paddled in the river together, she wanted to ask what came first in that song, love or warning. But he began talking about his family again. He had two sisters named Mary and Mercedes, both married, but his parents had died soon after he'd been notified about his scholarship, partly from the invisible, long-running wounds of the war. He mentioned only some of the traumas they'd witnessed: neighbours' heads impaled on fence railings by Japanese soldiers; young women forced into brothels for the Japanese invaders; terrible hunger and people dying of starvation on the streets. He told her that his father never revealed what he'd experienced as a prisoner of the Japanese in Changi Prison. But when he was finally released, his limbs were thin as sticks and his stomach bloated by beri-beri, and his screams during nightmares woke them for years after the war finished.

These were the only family traumas Francis could bring himself to tell Elspeth that evening. He hadn't told her yet that his father's wartime experiences had led to *Complications arising from alcoholism* written on his death certificate. Francis kept such family secrets underground.

'And you? You had a happy childhood down here, far away from the war?'

Should she tell him now about the imprecise recollection she'd had since early childhood of a huge shadow falling and obliterating her, and her apprehension that it might happen again? How could she justify telling him such a vague recollection, after his accounts of his suffering during the war and its long aftermath? He'd told her things about his past that made Elspeth feel both the water around her ankles and the pangs of sympathy in her body deepen. She missed the warnings altogether, and mistook them for love.

'Feel like a swim?' he asked, undoing the top buttons of his shirt.

The neat economy of his body. She lowered her eyes to her too-big knees and feet. 'I'll stay in the shallows. You go ahead.'

Waiting until he began freestyling towards the far end of the small wooden jetty, she pulled her dress off, leaving her underclothes on. Wrapped by darkness, she walked slowly through the shallows until it was just deep enough to float on her back.

Let go, she told herself, relaxing her arms and legs. *Let go,* she repeated, until the currents seemed to pass through her and she felt herself merge with the river. She floated with her overlapping reveries of him and the river until she thought she sensed him slowly returning, his strokes sending ripples through the dark water.

She scrambled to her feet to see he was only halfway between the jetty and her. Just enough distance to get dressed before he saw more of her than she felt ready to reveal.

※

When he invited her into his boarding house room, Francis showed Elspeth the yellowing ephemeris left in his parents' house by a British marine engineer returning to England on the eve of Singapore's Independence. This almanac gave the times and angles of sunrise and sunset, moonrise and moonset, for any date at various places in the world – but he couldn't find Perth in it. This made him suspect this city was one of the world's less significant places.

'Never mind, lah,' he said. 'At least Perth's part of the British Commonwealth.'

After living through the uncertainty of war, Francis had excelled at maths in high school, and appreciated precise measurements. Especially of light and time, since he had taken up photography as a hobby after finishing secondary school. His ephemeris divided both twilight and dawn into three phases and gave the precise times for each.

'Civil twilight,' he explained to Elspeth, 'falls when the sun's elevation is between zero and minus six degrees, when there's still enough light to see things clearly, and colour in the sky. Nautical twilight, when the sun's between minus six to minus twelve degrees. Astronomical twilight, when the sun's between minus twelve to minus eighteen degrees, and the sky appears almost totally dark.'

When Francis told Elspeth these mathematical facts during their courtship in Perth, she didn't find them incompatible with her own more literary interests. Life and the novels she'd read had already taught her that the story of a person's life might have its moments illuminated brightly, softly, or barely at all. And that persistent sense that her own life had long ago been shadowed by a shift in the late afternoon light, and something else besides. Something she couldn't articulate, something that resurfaced unpredictably as a searing pain behind her eyes, followed by indescribable darkness. Something that would affect her for the rest of her life.

※

On one of their evening walks along the river foreshore, Elspeth and Francis draw close to two black swans. An almost imperceptible sound comes from them.

'Is that just the sound their wing feathers make while they're preening?' Francis asks.

'No. They are communicating with each other,' Elspeth replies with more conviction than she actually feels. The river and sky darken suddenly as the sun dips below the limestone cliff downriver.

※

Elspeth's mother did not conceal her dismay when Elspeth told her on the phone that she had been seeing a student from Singapore for several months.

'Not one of those jolly Asians! Is he dark?'

'Yes.'

'How could you embarrass us like this? They come and live in our country but don't even have the decency to speak proper English. You never know what tropical diseases they might bring. Why can't you find a nice Australian boy? Or an Englishman like your father?'

'Because Francis is much more interesting than Australian and English boys,' Elspeth said, sighing as she recalled all her high school classmates planning to go to London after graduating. 'And Singapore sounds more interesting too.'

※

He becomes withdrawn and terse for days on end before exams and assignments are due, rushing to finish breakfast and conversations with her.

'If I fail, I lose my scholarship,' he explains before hurrying to the library, 'and get sent back to Singapore on the next boat.'

But just before their final exams, he asks her, over a hasty lunch of Vegemite on the boarding house's stale bread, to go with him to the university students' ball.

'Yes please!' she beams.

Not only because she'd always wanted to dance. She had

never learned ballroom dancing, and her mother had decreed her too plump to take ballet lessons as a child. All those suns setting over parched wheatbelt town creeks and opportunities denied. But also because of this river now widening and flowing towards the dazzling ocean and opportunities on distant shores she might share with him.

※

The day before the ball, Elspeth catches the bus from near the student boarding house to search in the department store sales for a suitable dress; clutching her purse with the envelope of birthday money her parents had mailed her.

It takes a few hours of searching through bigger sizes and dodging condescending saleswomen to find the velvet dress. Her favourite red, deep as blood. She already has a lipstick in that red, bought last year in defiance of her mother's pastels. Elspeth holds her breath in front of the Boans' department store changeroom mirror, exhaling with relief as the zip fastens easily enough over her waist. She does a full turn, imagines its skirt billowing as Francis spins her fast around the dance floor.

Just as difficult to find elegant shoes, her feet too wide and a childhood foot injury causing her pain when she tries on high heels. All that broken glass in that shallow salt-lake near her primary school.

She finally settles on a pair of low-heeled black velvet pumps, as close to wearing ballet slippers as she will ever come. Pulse racing with anticipation and almost missing the bus, she returns to the boarding house, her purchases rustling in their tissue-paper wrappings like a promise.

※

On the afternoon of the ball, she soaks in the rust-stained bathtub too long before dressing and piling her long hair into a high bun, puts too much make-up on before taking it off and starting again. It would be the first ball she and Francis had ever attended. This ball will be more than an opportunity to dance with him, she hopes. This might be the beginning of him leading her towards a new life.

※

Francis knocks on her door precisely fifteen minutes before the ball begins, just as she's dabbing at her lipstick with a tissue to make it a bit less intense. She hastily sprays her wrists and neck with perfume and slowly opens the door to him.

Unable to afford renting a tuxedo, he wears his deceased father's best suit and a bow tie. His wavy hair is slicked back with brilliantine. *Sleek as a seal,* she thinks as his dark eyes and mouth widen appreciatively at her appearance. She knows him well enough not to expect poetic words.

'Come. Don't want to be late lah,' he says finally. But he strokes her elbow-length sleeve and forearm with his fingers as they walk, tells her she looks like Audrey Hepburn but better fed. And he tells her he's never seen red velvet before;

because in Singapore, the weather is so hot most of the stores sell only cotton, linen and silk.

Does he notice the fine hairs rising on her arm when he touches it? After taking their seats in the hall, Francis keeps stroking Elspeth's velvet sleeve and forearm. She waits for him to ask her to dance but he remains seated, replying stoically to other students' questions about where he comes from and how long it had taken him to learn how to speak English. Her classmate Dianne looks them both up and down, runs her hands over her own much slimmer hips, smirking, as her blue-eyed date, a law student, leads her to the dance floor.

It isn't until just before the last dance, a waltz, that Francis confides in Elspeth, 'I don't know how to do that kind of dancing.'

They are the only ones still seated. She does not tell him she has attempted that kind of dance only once, at a cousin's wedding in a Country Women's Association hall in the wheatbelt, and that her partner there had been her father, who'd told her she'd have to lose some weight if she wanted to attract dance partners in future.

'We go now lah,' Francis says tersely, insistently.

'If you want,' she says, concealing her disappointment. 'Let's walk back along the river.'

They sidle out past the empty chairs, hoping their waltzing classmates don't notice them leaving early. They cross the road to the river but avoid the sandy shoreline, both of them worried about damaging their best shoes.

'Back home I've only done a Kristang folk dance called the branyo, at Eurasian weddings. It's much easier, you just join the line and follow the people in front of you.'

'I would like to do that dance with you one day in Singapore.'

He nods once and smiles tentatively. The river a black mirror reflecting the stars towards the Indian Ocean, a path away from everything she knows too well and wants to leave behind.

＊

He completes his engineering studies. The evening before he is due to return to Singapore, Francis takes Elspeth to eat fish and chips at Matilda Bay again. He has his Box Brownie camera with him.

Speaking less than usual, they eat quickly. Above them as they finish eating, two black swans head northwards through the sky.

'Maybe they're the same two swans we've seen here before,' she suggests. They hear the swans' call as they pass directly overhead.

'Is that a warning or some other kind of communication?' he asks.

'Maybe they're courting,' she tells him hopefully. 'I think they partner for life.'

'They're going in the direction of Singapore,' Francis says.

He pulls out his light meter. Measuring the light on

Elspeth's face, the river calm behind her. Each of them bodies of water, affected by how light and shadow fall on them at any given moment.

'The golden hour has nearly gone,' he tells her. Her heart skips a beat, thinking he is referring to how much he will miss her when he returns to Singapore. But as he continues, she realises he is revealing his knowledge of photography. 'It will be difficult to get enough depth of field to focus accurately on both your face and the river behind you.' He peers at her through his viewfinder. 'The light of any given day changes from minute to minute, hour to hour, heightening or flattening the colour and contours of the scenery,' he murmurs. A watcher of clouds' effects on sunlight since her childhood, she doesn't tell him she already knows this.

'Landscape photographers speak of the golden hour, the blue hour,' he explains more loudly, 'the golden hour occurs at dawn, and again at dusk. The blue hour occurs at both morning and evening twilights, when the sun is below the horizon but illuminating the upper layers of atmosphere. The longer red waves of light pass upwards into space; the shorter blue waves scatter through the atmosphere, turning the sky a cool, saturated blue.'

As he releases the camera's shutter button, she guesses the golden hour has passed into the blue already.

※

She caught the taxi with him to the harbour to farewell him early in the afternoon. The taxi came late. The driver raised his eyebrows at them and took the longer river route to Fremantle.

'Don't miss the boat lah,' Francis said, beads of sweat breaking out on his forehead.

'Going back to where you came from?' the driver asked, skidding to a halt outside the passenger terminal.

Francis didn't look at her as he hefted his suitcase towards the immigration officer's table. She put her arms around him after the officer had stamped his passport and ticket, but as the ship's boarding horn blasted, he'd already turned to walk up the ramp.

She wished she'd remembered to buy a paper streamer to grasp at one end and throw up to him as he stood at the ship's railing. Holding on to the end. Anything to prolong the connection with him. He waved just once to her as the vessel pulled out and swung out towards the ocean.

When the ship had disappeared from sight, she walked sobbing along the dock. She felt a desert growing inside as she found the footpath to the traffic bridge.

She'd reached the bottom of her well of tears by the time she'd walked to Port Beach. She saw a ship on the horizon heading north. Probably his. And then it disappeared, and there were only endless waves, breaking and spending themselves on the shore.

※

Shifting shadows

The light and shadow in her face come from somewhere besides the withdrawal of the day from the river on their final evening together. They come from her eyes, intense with grief, apprehension, yearning. Maybe even love.

Francis only notices all this after he gets his photograph of her printed in Wing's Photography Shop in Singapore.

LOSING TIME

FRANCIS returned to Singapore qualified as a water-supply engineer. On his first day at work, his English boss handed him a spade, a pair of rubber boots, a plan of the proposed sewerage system for a kampong near the CBD, a bottle of Jeyes disinfectant and a white cotton handkerchief to tie over his nose and mouth as he dug.

The ground around the kampong was like clay, and most of its inhabitants still emptied their urine, shit and food scraps from pots into open drains on the street, where they rotted alongside the occasional dead rat or seagull. His Australian university education hadn't prepared him to deal with these outpourings of human waste. He tied his own handkerchief over the one provided and tried not to breathe too deeply as early one morning he dug a tunnel for a new pipe between the stilts of a wooden kampong house.

He was unprepared for the sudden but short-lived

drenching of his head and shoulders that came from above, but recognised the smell of urine instantly.

'Ah *yah!*' he shouted. But whoever had emptied their night-waste over him had retreated indoors already. His heart hammered with alarm. Maybe disease was already entering his body. Cholera, hepatitis, God knows what else. He crossed and doused himself with water from his drink bottle and Jeyes disinfectant, and went directly to the government clinic for every inoculation he could get.

✻

That night, Francis dreamed of Hantu Maligang, the Malay ghost-demon of the underworld who comes up through the sewers to choose the next person, usually someone sick or dying, to drag down to the underworld. Francis shouted at Hantu Maligang to leave him alone, tried to push him back into the pool of raw sewage. But the demon, so long-haired and heavily bearded that Francis could not see his face, told him he had just returned from holidaying that night in one of the most beautiful and disease-free cities of the world below, and that he had met one of its most beautiful young women.

'Don't forget, you can't have a clean new city without sewers,' Maligang said as he disappeared below the sewage.

Francis woke certain that Hantu Maligang had been talking about Perth, where Elspeth Green and an efficient sewage disposal system were already in place, and cholera was almost non-existent. He wrote a letter inviting Elspeth to stay with him, stayed awake until the nearby Bukit Timah jungle's birds and gibbons began calling at dawn.

*

When Elspeth arrives at the Singapore docks a month later, Francis isn't there to greet her, despite her detailed telegram with her ship's arrival time. After her passport is stamped by an Indian man with a BBC accent, she searches in vain for Francis' face in the crowd. He'd been such a stickler for punctuality in Perth. He'll come any minute now, surely.

As the minutes pass, she becomes so entranced by the Chinese men on small red and green painted wooden boats ferrying vegetables and fruit to the next dock, their rattan bumpers nudging each other, that she doesn't notice she's the last passenger still waiting.

But as the other passengers leave in rickshaws and taxis, she sits on her suitcase and pulls her small bags closer, and feels her anxiety lengthen with the shadows of the godowns. What if he's changed his mind? Should she wait, or ask the few Australian crew on the dock about returning to Fremantle?

It's so hot, the neckline and short sleeves of her best summer dress stick to her skin, its blue and white rose print darkening. How much of it was perspiration, how much humidity? Panicking as a wave of dizziness rises, she pulls at the neckline. She's never been in this kind of humidity, and who can she ask for help?

Maybe her mother was right: it was way too risky to try

being with that man in this strange land. Despite winning the award for English Literature at university, Elspeth had withdrawn from her course to come and start a new life with Francis, but with no guarantees. Has she burnt all her bridges in Perth for nothing? She wonders if the university will allow her to re-enrol, if her parents will get over their disapproval of her decision to visit him here.

She sees a rickshaw approach from the far end of the dock, shadowed by the godowns. She doesn't see Francis in the passenger seat until he calls her name. Nearly two hours late. He alights, tells her that he had overlooked her arrival time because he'd been so busy working, and he'd taken off his cheap Phoenix-brand Chinese watch that morning so it wouldn't get dirty. The watch fell into one of the old open sewers. As it sank into the viscous liquid, he'd suddenly remembered her telegram.

Now, as they look at each other on the dock, she feels her sense of time has already started changing, after only minutes of being with him in his own country.

※

They restored their bond over two platefuls of longevity noodles from a nearby street hawker's barrow. And when Elspeth ran her fingers gently over his medal-shaped scars, Francis understood how wounds could transform into rewards.

※

He takes her to stay in his deceased parents' British colonial bungalow, which will soon be sold to developers. In the pre-monsoonal wind blowing through the wooden shutters of the bedroom, she senses her skin rippling under his touch, like light on water.

They wake at dawn to the rapturous cries of tropical birds and monkeys in the jungle nearby, and he throws open the shutters to reveal the garden where species from east and west mingle in the flourishing orchard grown by his parents and the long-departed English plantation owner.

※

When Elspeth becomes pregnant, Francis takes his sister Mercedes' advice. He goes to the Jewish-Armenian jeweller a few streets away from the church where he'd attended mass every Sunday with his family during his childhood before the war, and buys a pearl engagement ring because it didn't cost as much as a diamond one. He puts the ring in his pocket and takes Elspeth by rickshaw to the jungle near Bukit Timah Hill, the highest on the island.

'It's five hundred and eighty-one feet high,' he says, 'and this is the best primary evergreen tropical forest in the island. Raffles' banded monkeys still live there, and pangolins, and a rare mouse deer. That tree is a Dipterocarp nearly two hundred feet high. Botanists from all over the Commonwealth collect samples from here. Many of them are in the Kew Gardens in London.'

He points out the Tanglin and Tiong Bahru districts, where wealthy British and Chinese merchants had built their sprawling tropical bungalows amongst nutmeg plantations before they were engulfed by the expanding city; the airport runways being built around the only cell-blocks remaining from Changi Prison, where his father had been tortured by the Japanese.

As the gibbons and birds begin their evening songs in the jungle, the closest reservoir mirrors the red sun.

'Blood-red water,' she says.

Turning the ring over and over in his pocket, he decides against telling her about the Japanese soldiers' prostitutes who'd suicided near the reservoir at the end of the war.

※

'But he's *Asian*!' her mother remonstrated with her through the white noise of the long-distance phone call to Perth when Elspeth rang to tell her parents she was getting married. 'And dark.'

She couldn't bring herself to tell her mother that she was pregnant to him too.

※

Mercedes took her to Singapore's Little India for her wedding dress, directing the tailoress to make it several inches bigger around the waist because she ate too much.

The tailor laughed cynically. 'Memsahib like it spicy, no?'

Only his family came to the wedding, held in the mildewed white church beneath several plaster statues of Christ and Mary donated by their parents and other grateful parishioners who'd survived the war. Afterwards, they all feasted on longevity noodles and curry devil, and a two-tiered sugee cake Mercedes made from their mother's traditional Kristang recipe. Its icing was white, but its interior was a rich, granular yellow that melted in Elspeth's mouth.

'It's made from semolina. You have to break a lot of eggs and melt a lot of butter to get the recipe right,' Mercedes explained, and her husband Anthony winked at Francis and raised his eyebrows at Elspeth.

They do not dance the branyo, because there is no music.

※

No honeymoon followed. Francis and Elspeth shifted to the Pasir Panjang flats between the shoreline of the South China Sea and the power station, where Francis had taken a new, cleaner job. Pasir Panjang was Malay for 'long white beach'. The brick seven-storey block of flats had been built during the early years of Singapore's post-war reconstruction, inhabited by power-station employees and various English and European expatriates. The English expatriates directed the gardener to keep the jungle at a distance by maintaining a well-mown lawn around the apartments.

Elspeth missed the herbs she'd grown in her parents'

garden. When she was a child, her maternal grandmother had taught her their uses. Sage for making a calming tea. Mint for hot climate tea. Lavender for keeping moths away from woollens. Rosemary for roast lamb, and the final rinse of dark hair. And for remembrance.

✳

Francis gave Elspeth a crested yellow canary in a small wicker cage he'd bought from a Kristang colleague, to keep her company while he worked at the power station.

'She'll sing you Kristang songs of love,' he said. 'She's called Queenie, because of her crest.'

But in the following days, Elspeth tired of Queenie's limited repertoire, which contained mostly sharp tweets that sounded like warnings. The rarer sweet melody only lasted a few seconds.

✳

Elspeth began taking long walks. At first she kept to the long jungle-fringed beach, walking as far as the Pasir Panjang Forest Reserve near the entrance to the reconstructed harbour. She would watch the sampans rocking near the mouth of the river, the baby rocking in her womb. The map she carried of the nearby mangrove-lined inlets in Francis' 1957 *Singapore Street Directory* reminded her of the diagram of the human body's arteries she'd seen in the anatomy building in the university back in Perth. Everything led to the heart, everything sprang from the heart, it seemed. She felt her blood pulsing food and love to the baby in her own harbour.

A perfect tropical island, or so it seemed to her. You could lose yourself, yet you'd always find your way back home.

※

Sometimes on her way home from her walks, she stopped for a cup of tea at the Seaside Hotel, where labourers, expatriates and tourists drank Tiger Beer, Bombay Sapphire gin and Singapore Slings copied from the Raffles Hotel's recipe. But back at their flat on the fifth floor, Francis admonished Elspeth for roaming so dangerously.

'Ah-yah! That bar's as wild as the jungle. Not safe for a white woman to walk on her own anywhere around there lah!'

So Elspeth began catching buses towards the city centre. How desperate she was to find good food and faith. She ate nasi lemak at street hawkers' barrows and many kinds of noodles, in Chinese labourers' outdoor canteens that would have turned her parents' stomachs. She bought fabric and prayer mats at Arab Street and visited the nearby tomb of the Malay Princes in the old Malay Cemetery. She scrutinised the Raffles Museum's zoology, anthropology and prehistory collections; peered into intricate dioramas showing early Singapore's Malay villages, royalty and pirates, its British colonisation and Independence. In Lavender Road she watched the Chinese funeral decoration makers using bamboo and paper for replica houses, cars and effigies of recently deceased people, which they called zensheng, or true bodies. She bought British underwear and French perfume at Robinson's department store in Orchard Road, stopped in Little India's Sri Sivan Temple to pray under polished brass statues of elephant-trunked and multi-limbed gods and goddesses, before going around the corner to eat dhal and curry served on fresh banana leaves. She felt almost delirious with happiness: so many different ways to nurture body and soul within this small island's city.

※

Once in a Chinatown alley opposite a shop selling true bodies, a wizened old woman wearing a moth-eaten black silk jacket beckons to her and gently places her long-nailed forefinger on the mole at the corner of Elspeth's jaw.

'A sign of … unspeakable pain in infancy. You won't understand. Until you are old,' the fortune teller predicts.

'What do you mean?'

The fortune teller's eyes are sympathetic, but she simply shakes her head, over and over, until Elspeth bows and leaves.

※

In her third trimester of pregnancy, Elspeth's occasional migraine headaches intensified, sometimes accompanied by auras and bright white flashes. In the immediate aftermath of these auras and flashes, she sometimes saw strange people doing strange things. Once, on the edge of a kampong near the apartment she shared with Francis, she saw a wrinkled old Chinese woman with thin grey hair breastfeeding a newborn baby. Impossible, surely? She described them to my father after he returned home from work.

'People said there was a woman in that kampong who breastfed her grandson after his mother was killed during the war,' he said. 'But the old woman and the baby died a few months afterwards.'

The next evening, she told Francis when he returned from work that she'd seen an aging bald man in a sarong and white singlet sitting in Francis' father's carved plantation chair in their living room, drinking a whisky stengah.

'He sort of ... evaporated when I approached him.'

'Evaporated? Impossible lah! Describe him.'

'Stocky build. Same skin colour as yours. Thick eyebrows. Almost fierce expression on his face but he nodded at me and smiled before disappearing.'

Francis's eyes widened behind his square-framed spectacles and his voice trembled slightly. 'My father looked like that. He used to sit in that chair after he changed out of his harbour officer's uniform into a sarong after work. Many Singaporeans believe in ghosts. But not any British or Australian expatriates I know.' He paused. 'So why are you not like other white women, lah?' he asked. 'Why do you see ghosts?'

Elspeth did not know how to answer that question.

One of Francis' photographs of Elspeth in Singapore showed a bright white person-shaped flare behind her, its profile apparently looking out through the French doors towards the South China Sea. But the flare obliterated any identifying features.

'Must be one of the ghosts you saw,' he joked.

'Maybe it is.'

'Nonsense lah. You can't photograph ghosts. A ghost image like this is common in the tropics when you're shooting into bright light. It's just a phantom image, most likely of the camera's lens diaphragm itself.'

※

Her Singaporean ghost images

Elspeth's deceased father-in-law sits in the old teak planter's chair, wearing a sarong and a white singlet, legs akimbo on the shin-rests as he sips from his whisky stengah, its fumes apparently rising from the glass until he seems to dissolve in them.

Her deceased mother-in-law, identifiable by the goitre on her neck and her Indian tailor's copy of a New Look dress covered by a matching kebaya, offers a rich yellow piece of cake on a plate to my mother, but disappears before she can take it.

The deceased Chinese grandmother on the edge of the nearby kampong breastfeeds the newborn baby wrapped in the front flap of her white sam-foo tunic. Clear as daylight, but the closer my mother draws, the fainter their image becomes.

These images of dead Singaporeans Elspeth had never seen before. They appear to her just once each during her pregnancy, as vividly as if they are alive, before fading until it seems they'd never been there at all.

OTHER KINDS OF DEVELOPMENT

MY mother-to-be panted her way through her contractions in the labour ward of Kandung Kerbau maternity hospital.

'Kandaung Kerbau translates as Pregnant Ox,' Dr Lee the obstetrician told her, trying to take her mind off the pain. Between contractions, she heard the machinery of the new Singaporean government's builders across the road, replacing the old kampongs with multistorey apartment blocks. Finally, when the contractions came so frequently that she could only hear her own panting, I sailed out on a red tide between her legs.

'Well,' announced Dr Lee, 'it's not a boy, but she's a beautiful baby. Birth weight eleven pounds. Probably a record for this hospital. And a good healthy pair of lungs.' He handed me to my mother.

'Listen to that,' my father said proudly. 'She's bringing good news.'

'We'll have to name her Evangelia,' my mother said. 'It means bringer of good news.'

'Evangelia Oliveira. Where's Oliveira from?' asked Doctor Lee.

'My parents are descendants of Portuguese-Eurasians from Malacca,' said Francis. 'Oliveira means olive tree in Portuguese. From an ancestor who sailed with Captain Albuquerque to Malacca during the Portuguese Age of Expansion in the sixteenth century.'

'Ah, so you're one of the in-between people, as the British would say. And you, Elspeth?'

'Born in Australia,' my father said when she didn't reply. 'Her parents are mostly English, a bit Scottish, and a bit French.'

'So many races swimming around in your baby's gene pool!' said Doctor Lee, patting my mother on the hand. 'No wonder she's so strong and healthy, Elspeth.'

But my sudden fierce first suck on my mother's breast had silenced her.

※

My mother continues to breastfeed me when she returns from the hospital, much to the consternation of her sister-in-law.

'So unhygienic lah!' Mercedes says, brandishing magazine advertisements for Nestlé's infant formula. But my mother persists, sticking to the skin of her slightly darker-skinned baby by Singapore's humidity.

※

My parents had me immunised against every possible tropical disease. The skin on my dimpled bottom puckered into tiny rosettes around the needle puncture sites, confirming my father's view that I was an award-winning baby.

※

Still a member of the Singapore Amateur Photographers' Club, my father bought a twin-lens camera from a British engineer returning to England in the wake of Singapore's Independence and began his longest-running photographic project. He used black and white film only, because it didn't cost so much to develop and print.

※

My father's new family album

Me swaddled in my mother's arms.

Me in the plastic Chinese baby bath, my legs too long for it.

Me on the kitchen scales.

Me in a small round rattan armchair several months later, my face obscured by the English nursery rhyme picture books abandoned by the previous tenants, expatriates who'd returned to the mother country.

Me naked under the palm tree shade alongside the South China Sea, the centre of attention, my mother and Aunty Mercedes laughing at me together, despite their differences. My mother's pale limbs and face so full compared to my petite Eurasian aunt's, but the shadow in her smile darker.

A GREAT FALL

MY mother nourished me throughout my early childhood not only with milk and carefully prepared food, but with stories of where I'd come from, who I was and who I might yet become. Years later, some of them seem as wondrous and improbable as miracles, especially the one about my great fall.

※

Grown so plump by my second year that my uncle called me Humpty Dumpty, and soon after I began walking, I have my miraculous fall. On the balcony of our fifth floor flat at Pasir Panjang, I climb a rattan chair beneath our wicker-caged yellow canary, Queenie. What was I looking for?

In the bathroom, my mother doesn't notice Queenie tweeting more warnings than usual. I escape my nappy. Like a Houdini protégé, I straddle the balcony railing and tip over its edge.

As Queenie tweets in alarm, I fall past the multi-armed brass goddess on our Indian neighbours' balcony and the incense offerings on the balconies of our Chinese neighbours, hit the frangipani-strewn lawn with a thud louder than the coconuts make when they fall from the nearby tree. So loud that my mother hurries from the bathroom to find me gone from the balcony. Only my nappy hanging – still firmly safety-pinned – from the balcony railing. Seeing me spread-eagled and unmoving on the lawn below, my mother runs shouting down the stairs, followed by the Indian couple who had seen me fall.

'We pray memsahib! We pray!'

Still I do not move, not one bit. Not even to breathe. My mother picks me up and sobs over my limp body. The French expatriate woman on the ground floor runs out and yells to her: 'Beat the demons out of her!' She demonstrates with five hard slaps to my back, but it isn't until my mother kisses me goodbye, tears streaming down her face, that I cry and breathe again.

But my behaviour in the following months and in the years ahead, shows that not all the demons were beaten from me.

※

Many of our neighbours believed in ghosts and demons. Our Chinese neighbours lit incense and left food for their ancestral ghosts at the small red and gold shrine next to their green front door. Our Malay neighbours left sharp nails, pieces of glass, and pineapples on their threshold and windowsills to snare any demons who might try to enter their home.

Over the following year, I ate the offerings of crackers and salted preserved plums our Chinese neighbours next door left for ghosts, and souvenired shiny pieces of glass from our Malay neighbours. And I began mimicking them all, my aunt's, parents' and our various neighbours' speech.

'Ah yah man! What lah?' I shout at Aunty Mercedes when we visit her and my uncle in the apartment on the next floor down.

'What you damn well doing?' I ask the English couple from the flat next door when we meet them on the stairs.

'Bon-joo! Voulay voo-oo-oo?' I sing to the French woman who helped save my life.

'Gong-ee fat choy-nese man!' I shout at the Chinese couple, months after Chinese New Year has passed.

'Boleh? Tidak boleh!' I exclaim to the Malay family. 'Can lah? Cannot!'

※

My father and Aunty Mercedes inherited very little from their parents, because their oldest sister Mary had married a rogue Chinese man who sold their parents' house to developers and pocketed the money, soon after my parents married. The developers bulldozed it to build a multistorey shopping centre to service Lee Kuan Yew's Housing Development Board multistorey apartments nearby, where residents of entire kampongs had been relocated. Such unprecedented feats of engineering, both physical and social!

Mindful of his new family, my father anxiously watched public service job opportunities for Singapore's Eurasian minority diminishing as Lee Kuan Yew's government swept out the deadwood and the yellowing contracts left behind by the British.

⁕

The small apartment felt more and more constrained to my mother as I grew bigger and bigger, but it was too difficult in the hot tropical sun to take me in my pram onto buses, especially as my father deemed the walk to the closest bus stop on the edge of some remnant jungle too far and unsafe. Besides, the power station was close enough for him to walk back for lunch, saving money, he pointed out to my mother, and providing her with company.

But despite her diligent efforts to be a good mother and wife, the hours either side of lunch soon felt as claustrophobic to her as the apartment. She knew no-one nearby with infants, and by my second year, her lonely daily routine of providing breakfast, lunch and dinner for my father made her days and the view across the South China Sea look desolate and endless.

⁕

Returning home after work one evening, my father found my mother slamming doors, crying with frustration.

'I feel trapped in this place. I need more freedom and space. Eva does too.' She didn't know how much she wanted to return to Australia until she heard herself say these words.

'Tidak boleh! Cannot, lah! Shrinking horizons!' he replied.

But their hopes grew when they received a letter from Elspeth's father saying that Western Australia needed water supply surveyors and engineers. The next morning, my father told my mother he'd dreamed of the demon Maligang again.

'He told me to go to Australia, the New World. And not to forget him, that my destiny was in the sewers of Perth and that I would need him. He told me, There is no new world without an underworld.'

'What a wonderful dream. Maybe it's an omen,' my mother suggested.

That day, my father wrote to his father-in-law and asked him to make enquiries with the Australian Immigration Department about the prospect of them migrating and him getting a job there. A few weeks later, his father-in-law wrote to say he'd made enquiries, but it seemed Francis' dark Asianness would be incompatible with the White Australia Policy.

※

My mother finds a turban shell when we walk together along the long white hem of the South China Sea below our apartment. She holds it to my ear.

'Listen,' she says. 'Can you hear the sea?' But I hear only her breathing and mine. Waiting.

※

My parents' dream of living in Australia seems to recede far from their reach. But my Perth grandfather eventually pulls some tangled strings that move rubber stamps somewhere in the Western Australian Public Service and the Australian Immigration Department. Permission to migrate finally comes through several months after, when some other mysterious Australian authority clears my father.

'Probably Australian government spies, checking out my Communist Party membership here after I finished high school,' my father mutters. 'That happened to one of my friends.'

※

'What's Mummy doing?' I asked as I watched her pack our clothes in five Great Wall brand suitcases my father bought for a bargain price from Chinatown. She carefully folded her wedding dress, veil and magenta silk shawl into the smallest one.

'Getting us ready to go on a big aeroplane.'

She used the local Chinese newspaper's death notices to wrap my father's family photo albums, his mother's blue floral porcelain pickle jars, the large granite mortar and pestle called a toomba-toomba, the enormous earthenware Shanghai bathing pot and his classical records, placing them carefully into wooden tea chests. She hid two bulbs of lemongrass beneath the Mozart symphonies and Beethoven concertos nestled in the Shanghai pot. The faces of recently deceased Singaporean-Chinese grandparents stared accusingly at her from the calligraphic newsprint.

'We fly?'

'To Australia.'

It sounded like ostrich to me. My book of animals had a picture of a bird hiding its head in the sand. Was that where we were going?

✳

'Ostrich? When we going to Ostrich?' I ask each morning over breakfast. 'Tomorrow?'

'Just a few more tomorrows,' my mother replied every day as she fed me boiled egg or kaya coconut jam on toast. 'Wait and see.'

✳

Aunty Mercedes buys me two dolls from Little India, one with a black felt face and body, dressed in striped trousers and a blue waistcoat; the other pale pink felt and wearing a silk dress made from red and gold sari remnants.

'Mummy and Daddy,' she beams. 'They're not really dressed for the colder weather in Australia though.'

'Let's hope they get used to it quickly,' Dad says.

'I'm looking forward to having winter again,' Mum says.

'I hope it doesn't make Francis and Evangelia sick,' Aunty Mercedes mutters, her voice a bit anxious, a bit sad, a bit angry.

※

'Today!' my father finally announces to me over a breakfast of toast spread with the last scrapings of *kaya* jam from the jar.

'At long last!' my mother smiles at me.

'It will make us stronger and healthier,' says my father.

'How?'

'Like magic,' he promises me.

※

Aunty Mercedes and Uncle Anthony agreed to take care of Queen Elizabeth in her wicker cage. They waved us off from the new airport terminal built on the Changi Prison site. My father took one last photo before we waved to them for the last time and hurried through our final doorway from Singapore.

※

Circling for the last time in the jet plane above Singapore before ascending further, my mother pointed out to me the East Lagoon's palm trees, black against the pink dawn sky; the Chinese traders loading their brightly painted tongkang boats near the harbour; the British ships sunken by the Japanese on the eastern edge of the mangrove-fringed lagoon, and far away now, Pasir Panjang beach. We didn't know then that the island's shoreline we'd looked at every day from our apartment window would soon be lost to land reclamation forever, that the maps in my father's 1957 *Singapore Street Directory* would be useless next time we saw Singapore.

The plane carried us through fairy floss pink clouds above the South China Sea, towards the Indian Ocean and more empty space than I'd ever seen before. And another kind of fall that would end again on an unknown land below, but this time a land that I'd never known.

※

Last snapshot of Singapore

Farewell at Changi Airport's terminal gate: waving goodbye with all the strength in my skinny three-year-old body to Aunty Mercedes, tears coursing down her face. Behind her, gleaming plate-glass windows framing the centuries old kampongs and rainforested hills, a fast-receding backdrop to the construction of shining new apartments for the ones who stayed behind.

Years of
Drifting Apart

FAMILY ASSORTED

THE accents of our new Australian neighbours barbecuing their weekend lunch were more difficult to comprehend than our apartment neighbours in Singapore. Their elongated vowels and drink-slurred words came to us across greater distances and seemed untranslatable to me.

'Giddaaay ya old bastard! Howya bloody goin'?'

'See ya got new neighbours.'

'Some kinda wog.'

'What are they saying?' I asked my parents.

'Oh, it's just white noise,' my father replied cryptically, lowering the needle on a Mozart concerto on his old teak-boxed record player from Singapore before making his weekend curry.

※

The suburban Perth birdcalls sounded different to Singapore's birds too, as raucous, squawky and gravelly as our new neighbours' voices.

'Why do the birds here talk different?'

'Different birds. Different species of plants and animals. Perth is dryer than Singapore,' my mother said.

'In more ways than one,' my father muttered.

'Will the birds sing different if they have more to drink?'

'Probably not.'

'I can't hear any monkeys,' I said.

'No monkeys here.'

'Apart from the neighbours, lah,' my father said loudly. My mother turned up the volume on the soprano singing on the ABC radio.

Sometimes, between the end of the presenter's talk and the next piece of music, I thought I heard fainter radio signals from much farther away, and imagined they were from Dad's extended family in Singapore, transmitting messages about our connections to Asian royalty and other famous people.

'Who are you?' a girl called out as she walked past me in our front garden. 'And why do you look so strange?'

'I am a princess from another land far away.'

'You wanted to be so much more to our neighbours than just an unknown foreign girl,' my mother concluded when she reminded me of this incident years later.

※

Our neighbours mostly kept to their blond-brick suburban houses and backyards. I took up spying and eavesdropping. They seemed to talk most often about football, cricket and fishing, but one weekend I heard a visitor speaking to the man next door.

'What're your new neighbours like?'

'Don't know much about them. But they're from Singapore, and he's a darkie.'

'Really?' the visitor responded.

In the silence that followed, my face felt as if it was burning. I ran inside and grabbed a handful of Arnott's Family Assorted biscuits while my parents weren't looking, sidled into my bedroom and ate them, to replace the neighbour's words with something sweeter.

My mother later told me that those first months after we migrated were like the beginning of my own Age of Expansion. All those new Australian challenges and new foods to conquer. All that emptiness to fill.

*

From a family of keen gardeners, my mother didn't waste much time on the eclectic scramble of remnant bush and English species in our front yard: a bed of Peace roses and scraggly kikuyu grass under an old jarrah tree, hydrangeas in the more shaded bed against the house. But in the backyard's rockery in which only a few abandoned succulents grew, she propagated slips of rosemary, mint, thyme and lavender from her parents' garden and germinated seeds of sweet basil in a large discarded laundry copper. She planted rhubarb in the small orchard of orange and mandarin trees near the back fence. And the bulbs of lemongrass from the Singaporean tea chest.

My parents looked in vain through the Perth nurseries for mango, lime and papaya trees, but found a small Eureka lemon tree they planted in our Singaporean earthenware Shanghai pot patterned with serpentine Chinese dragons riding waves and clouds. The pot's glaze cracked in the drier heat of our first Perth summer, so that it soon looked to me like an antique relic from some fantasy land that seemed to be thousands of miles and years away.

❋

When he couldn't fix a blockage in our drains and toilet simply, my father knew where to dig to find the sewage tank.

'Much easier to dig through this dry soil than Singapore's clay,' he pronounced. I watched, fascinated, from the edge of the hole he'd dug. 'Stand back,' he shouted through the handkerchief tied over his nose and mouth, 'or Hantu Maligang will drag you down into the underworld. Last time I dug a hole this deep in Singapore, he took my watch.' He found the sewer blocked by enormous thirsty eucalyptus and wattle tree roots, chopped them away with his shovel.

'Why does it smell so bad?'

'It's sewage. Caca and sisi.'

'Why's the water grey instead of brown like caca?'

'Maybe the previous owners were English. Paler bodies might make paler caca,' he winked. Glancing down, he suddenly shifted his foot and grabbed a tree root to stop from falling. 'Ah yah!' he exclaimed. 'A scorpion! See it? Much bigger than the ones in Singapore! Poisonous.' The creature moved slowly towards his foot, tail-sting raised. My father pushed it into the sewage with his shovel. A few drops of sewage splashed his hand. He wiped it hastily on his overalls and scrambled quickly back up the hole, beads of sweat on his brow. 'Hantu Maligang must've sent it to drag me back into the underworld,' he muttered, shovelling the dry Perth earth quickly back over the sewage. 'Elspeth!' he yelled, 'bring the Jeyes quickly!'

Mum rushed through the back door with a bottle of Jeyes disinfectant and a cup of Milo. Provident, the saviour he'd dreamed she was before he married her.

'What's wrong, Love?' she asked him. When she called him that, it always sounded like it had a capital L.

'I got some sewage on my hand,' he said. 'And there was a scorpion, much bigger than I've ever seen. Killed it though.'

'Brave Love,' she said, pouring the Jeyes disinfectant onto his trembling outstretched hand.

'It's like Maligang told me in the dream before we left Singapore,' my father said to her. 'You can't have a clean new world on top without the old underworld below.'

※

That year, I often dreamed of falling. Sometimes I fell past our Singaporean Chinese neighbours leaving chicken rice, incense and other offerings on their balcony for the Hungry Ghosts; sometimes past the kind Indian neighbours leaning and reaching out like the multi-armed gods and goddesses I'd seen in the temple in Little India, powerless to catch me. Sometimes past the red-faced expatriate Englishman in his Bombay Bloomers sharing a Tiger beer with another expatriate. Or I sank through the sewers like Maligang the demon, to the deepest recesses of the underworld, where Singapore's sewers flowed and joined Australia's. Or I fell from a jet plane as I ate a small bucket of Peters ice-cream, fell past Queenie the canary, singing her heart out in her wicker cage at our Pasir Panjang balcony, all the way to the depths where the South China Sea met the Indian Ocean.

Other times, these dreams included scenes from my new life. I fell past our new Australian neighbours barbecuing sausages and chops, most of the men too drunk to do anything but stare as I fell past. And after my Anglo-Australian grandfather read me *Alice in Wonderland*, I dreamt of falling like Alice down a rabbit hole and meeting a pinkish-white rabbit who spoke with a BBC English accent. But always these dreams seemed so terrifyingly real that I'd be glad to wake with a jolt, just before I hit the bottom. The magpies calling outside reassured me I was still alive, despite being in this new country that sometimes seemed stranger than dreams.

※

On the weekends my parents sometimes cooked together, flavouring their curries with lemongrass from the garden. But they couldn't buy any of the other spices they'd bought at the Singapore markets. They made do with Keen's Curry Powder for the first five years. And Maggi two-minute noodles were as close as we could get to longevity noodles.

'These will shorten our lives,' my father said glumly the few times we ate them.

※

Mornings in our earliest years in Australia, my mother emerged like the sun from between the orchard and gumtrees, her hands and new hot-pink and lime green Marimekko apron's pocket full of fresh herbs she'd gathered for dinner. Basil, sage, thyme and rosemary for a recipe from her recently purchased Elizabeth David's Mediterranean cookbook, or lemongrass for a curry.

'Take a deep breath, Eva. Can you smell them? Australia and Singapore and Europe all in one garden.' Smiling at sharing with me those exotically scented moments of light and shade in our suburban Western Australian garden.

※

My father brought home a cheeping cardboard box the size of a book. My mother lifted the lid to reveal six baby chickens. We put them in a small pen my father built in the corner of the orchard and fed them our meal scraps in the morning, everything from Kellogg's Cornflakes to scrapings of curry and rice.

The chickens grew over two seasons to fully fledged chooks and ranged freely over the backyard, fertilising it with their cross-cultural shit. One of them climbed the wattle tree to lay her eggs, which landed on the concrete path below, sometimes narrowly missing the heads of unsuspecting people.

'Curried egg,' my mother said once when she smelled a smashed egg cooking on the sun-heated path.

❈

Our first winter in Australia, I developed asthma, especially at night.

My mother filled my old enamel baby bath with hot water and a dash of eucalyptus oil, held a blanket over my head and the tub as I inhaled the steam during my first serious asthma attack.

'Breathe,' she says calmly, holding my hand. Her voice, soft and gentle as the night.

'Should've bought Tiger Balm from Singapore lah,' my father said as I wheezed feebly, sobbing in the steam. Even more humid than eating laksa in cramped Singaporean tearooms and not at all tasty. 'And Mercedes, to pray to God for us all.'

❈

The next day, my mother bought me warm flannelette pyjamas printed with yellow ducklings, some pink furry slippers and a picture book about a baby goose with no feathers whose mother knitted a jumper for her instead.

God bless you, the mother goose said near the end of the book.

'What is God?' I asked Mum after she finished reading the book to me at bedtime.

'Ah,' she said calmly, gently. 'That's something you'll need to find out for yourself. Different people have different gods, and some have none at all.'

My mother slept badly through those Western Australian months of asthma, anxiety and eucalyptus vapours, but did not falter in front of me. I extorted new books and clothes from her before inhaling her painstakingly prepared eucalyptus steam and forgetting all about God.

※

With her encouragement, I taught myself to read the newspapers when I was four and a half.

'*Do we want a nation of coffee-coloured Australians?*' I read to my astonished grandfather this caption from beneath *The West Australian* newspaper cartoon of slant-eyed people mingling with sunburned blonds. Apparently speechless, he did not answer the question.

※

Anzac Day in Perth. Recently turned five years old, I reclined with the family in deckchairs on my grandparents' carefully mown lawn, between their Eureka lemon tree and the Loo Bloo-tinted birdbath, eating scones and Arnott's Family Assorted biscuits, drinking Weaver and Lock lemonade while the adults drank Swan Lager shandies. Grandpa and Grandma Green had silver hair and pale wrinkled skin and echoes of their English childhoods in their voices.

When the side gate squeaked, Grandma Green sat up straight under her stiffly permed hair.

'Here comes your Uncle Arthur. A war hero. He fought in Singapore,' she said proudly. Why did my mother's grip on my hand tighten as the balding war hero approached, baring his nicotine-stained teeth? 'Say hullo to your Great-Uncle Arthur, Evangelia.'

I refused, burying my face in Mum's lap.

'Did the Japs send you to Changi?' Dad asked Arthur affably.

'I got out of Singapore in the nick of time,' Uncle Arthur replied. 'So what bullshit yer up to?'

'Working as a water supply and sewage disposal engineer for the Western Australian Government,' my father replied proudly.

'Sounds like a load of shit,' quipped Uncle Arthur with a smirk. 'Bloody stealing Aussies' jobs, you Asians.' He turned away from my father and bent over me. I smelled his tobacco-and-beer breath. 'Funny you should have a daughter like her,' he murmured to Mum. 'Quite pretty. She'll grow up to look like one of those Singapore nightclub hostesses, just a bit paler.'

The war medals on his flabby chest swung in my face.

※

My father read the glaring Western Australian sunshine in different locations over the next few years, divining new photographic projects with his old hand-held light meter from Singapore. He measured the light, then photographed us with his twin-lens camera, experimenting with different exposures. He photographed us at home, in my grandparents' garden, in Kings Park and at Port Beach, where we watched ships depart and arrive from all over the world. We built sandcastles as summer's light elongated into the evenings, before slowly contracting over the months with the cool air of autumn and winter, both colder than any season we'd had in Singapore.

※

The national newspaper only mentioned Perth regularly on its weather page. Most of its stories were about Sydney, Melbourne and Canberra.

'Does that mean Perth news isn't very important?' I asked Mum as we sat on the verandah reading the newspaper.

'No. Maybe the Eastern States newspaper owners think we're so far away we're almost in another world,' she replied.

'A boring world,' I grumbled, glancing at the one-storey brick houses stretching as far as I could see.

'Or maybe we're all just not looking hard enough,' she suggested.

'At what?'

'Whatever lies under the surface of this place.'

※

But a few days later, as my parents argued in low voices in the kitchen about something I couldn't quite hear, something made my bed and floor shake so much that I thought we might be about to fall far below the surface, maybe even into the underworld. Maybe soon, our new neighbours would forget we ever existed. I hid under my pink chenille bedspread until my mother came looking for me.

'Are we still here?' I asked her, peeling back the cover cautiously.

'Yes.'

'Did your fight with Dad make the house shake?'

'No. It was just a little argument. But the radio's saying we've had a small earthquake.'

'What's that?'

'It's when two parts of the earth collide under the surface.'

'Is it dangerous?'

'Probably not when it's small like this one.'

'At last! We're in the news!' I jumped out of bed. She took me by the hand.

'Just to be safe, we need to get away from the house for a few minutes.'

She led me with Dad to the orchard, where the ripe oranges had fallen early to the ground and the magpies and parrots finished their short-lived songs of warning.

※

Appalled at the cost of printing photos in Perth compared to Mr Wing's Photography Shop on the edge of Singapore's Chinatown, Dad reverted to using black and white film so he could print our family photos himself. He bought a small black film-developing tank, trays and enlarger.

On my way from the toilet late one Saturday night, I heard a mysterious whirring and liquid sloshing from behind the locked bathroom door. Putting my eye to the keyhole, I saw my father bent over a tray of water, lit dimly by a small red light in the darkness. Its reflections rippled across his face. He looked as if he was subjecting his skin to some strange metamorphosis. Was this the beginning of the transformation he'd promised me on the eve of our departure from Singapore? Or perhaps he was trying to make himself paler.

'What are you doing in there?' I shouted through the key-hole.

'I'm printing my photos,' he shouted back. 'Go to bed. I need to cover the keyhole too, so no light gets in.'

'Daddy's turned the bathroom into a darkroom,' Mum called from the kitchen, as if that explained the whole mystery.

'Wash your hands in the laundry and hop back into bed.'

When I finally fell asleep, I dreamed of the skin on my father's face and mine, burning and peeling away in front of our Australian neighbours and Uncle Arthur. I shouted to them, *Look! Ours is the same colour blood as yours*, but none of them heard or looked.

※

Newly exposed

My father's latest black and white photographs hang on the washing line between his strip of negatives and our underpants.

In the negatives, I see Mum and my white-toothed smiles transformed into gaping black holes and our dark hair into glowing white haloes.

And the prints, easier to read and understand:

Portraits of me smiling gap-toothed from beneath a bad haircut I'd done with the kitchen scissors behind the fridge when no-one was watching.

Building sandcastles on the shores of the Indian Ocean at an empty Port Beach in autumn, rugged up against the unfamiliar Perth cold in our new woollen jumpers, a circle drawn in the sand around each one of us. As if we were each in our own little world.

WRONG KIND OF YELLOW

'YOUR skin was sort of *yellow* before you tanned. Why?' one of the grade three Debbies asked me in the school playground in my first week of grade one.

'She's Chinese,' another Debbie suggested.

'Why do you turn brown instead of red or pink in the sun? Now you're nearly the same colour as Colin.'

I didn't reply. Colin was the only Aboriginal person in our class. I had a secret crush on him, a sense of kinship because, like me, he had a brown father and a pale mother. Colin and I both agreed that the large brown snails in the school garden were males and the small white ones were females. I didn't know they were actually two different species of snail.

'And why do you have that funny name?' the second Debbie asked.

'My real name is Sally Jones and I was a princess back in the land where I was born,' I yelled.

Back home that afternoon, I asked Mum:

'Am I white, yellow or brown? Or pink?' I added hopefully.

'You're sort of somewhere in between all those colours, depending on whether you've been out in the sun long. Always a beautiful colour. You're *Eurasian*.'

She made Eurasian sound like something rare. But I wanted to be a pinkish white girl who sunburned to red, just like the other girls at school, and to have hair that bleached to blonde.

※

A few weeks after beginning school, I told my parents I wanted a more Australian name.

'We should've called you Big Mouth,' my father teased as he completed the Australian citizenship application form. 'Because you eat and talk too much.'

'Ssshh,' I said, 'my ears are aching.'

'Rubbish lah,' said my father. 'You've just been eavesdropping too much. Evangelia the eavesdropper.'

'You don't believe me! Okay then, my name is Sally Jones!' I shouted, covering my ears with my hands.

※

Over our first few years in Australia, something made holes in the two felt dolls Aunty Mercedes had bought me in Little India.

'Oh dear,' my mother said. 'Probably just wear and tear. They're a bit thin-skinned and the stuffing's been knocked out of them.' She re-plumped them with scraps of merino wool fleece from my grandparents' sheep-farming friend, and patched them with fabric from her old Singaporean dresses and a pair of Dad's old chino trousers.

But something made holes in them even faster over the next few months. My mother found a silver wing near one of the holes.

'Ah! Of course, I'd forgotten how much Australian moths like wool,' she declared. 'Do you want me to repatch them with cotton?'

'No. I've grown out of those mother and father dolls,' I declared imperiously. 'I want a blonde Barbie doll wearing a bikini.'

※

That summer, my mother fainted in front of me for the first time. Shocked by how pale she looked as she lay on the grey linoleum kitchen floor, I shouted as loudly as I could: 'Wake up Mummy!' She took too long to open her eyes, and seemed not to recognise me at first. I grabbed her hands and pulled as hard as I could. My first attempt at trying to bring her back into the world again.

※

One morning early that autumn, I wake to the sound of the milkman placing bottles on the front doorstep. I run from my bed to the step to collect the bottles of milk, as usual. But what I see instead is not usual.

My mother, lugging a suitcase towards the end of our street, almost out of my sight. I follow at a distance, my heart pounding, until she reaches the corner.

'Mummy! Where are you going?' I shout, trying to cover the distance between us with my voice. But she doesn't turn or reply. Even when I'm close enough for her to hear, she keeps her back turned to me. Even when I run right up to her and tap her on the arm. 'Isn't that too heavy for you to carry? I'll help if you come back!'

Finally she turns around. '*Ssshh!* Okay. Let's go home,' she murmurs, sighing. She's wearing her darkest sunglasses, so I can't see her eyes.

'My legs are aching,' I whine.

'We'll get there soon. Not far to go now.' What she always said when we went on long walks. The suitcase slows her down, but I don't run ahead of her. Because who knows what she'll do if I let her out of my sight?

❋

After, my mother drank more cups of tea and coffee than ever in the morning.

'Why do you drink so many?'

'To get me going,' she'd say.

'Where? You're not allowed to go away without me again,' I'd say. 'Promise.'

'Promise.' Unsmiling, her eyes lowered. Sometimes she'd turn her back on me. Finding no words to remedy this, I'd hug her, but she did not smile. I'd offer her all the money in my piggybank, but still she did not smile. I would do anything to make her smile, but had no idea what would.

✳

At school, I pretended often to be sick in the following weeks, hoping the teacher would call my mother to come pick me up. It wasn't just that I missed her. It was because I was worried about her and sensed that *she* was sick, in some way I couldn't understand.

My kind young teacher took me to the sick-room, where I waited for my mother to pick me up and begin the long walk home.

✳

A couple of months later, Aunty Mercedes flew from Singapore on a cut-price flight. She brought with her lengths of fabric from Arab Street and a large packet of salted preserved plums wrapped in white paper printed with green calligraphy beneath a drawing of a cargo ship and a fruit tree.

'Ah! Cheng Pi Mai brand,' my father said approvingly, unwrapping one and sucking noisily on it. *'Saudade.* Remember after the war was over and we tasted these again for the first time? Just looking at them made us salivate, even after we'd eaten a big meal.'

I unwrapped one. It looked like a kangaroo dropping, but as soon as I put it on my tongue, my saliva flowed, my lips puckered and images of a small red and gold shrine near a green door rose behind my closed eyelids. Back to an almost forgotten bliss.

I sucked all the flavour from it until nothing remained but its seed. While the adults weren't looking, I pocketed a handful of the plums, taking care to leave just a few for each of them. I took them to my bedroom, sucked on a few more and stored the rest with the brunette Barbie doll with the bandaid-coloured skin that Grandma Green had given me for my birthday.

'Nearly the same colouring as you,' she'd explained as I struggled to conceal my disappointment at the doll's lack of blondeness, 'only a bit paler.'

※

Aunty Mercedes only visited for a week, but she helped with the housework and the cooking every day, and glanced sidelong at Mum often. Unlike my mother, she went to something called Mass in the local church early every morning, rarely sitting longer than five minutes over her single morning cup of tea before she left.

When we took Aunty Mercedes to my grandparents' house, we had afternoon tea with scones, jam and cream and Schweppes lemonade for me, before playing an idiosyncratic kind of cricket on my grandfather's meticulously mown lawn of Queensland Blue couch grass. Then my father put his twin-lens camera on a tripod to take group photographs of us with my Aunty Mercedes in the garden. With his hand-held light meter, he took a long time reading the light on our faces.

'So many different skin colours. Photographing us all together,' he explained, 'compromises have to be made with the exposure. Not so little light that the darker faces' details disappear. Not so much light that the palest faces look like ghosts.' He put the shutter on delayed release and ran to join us for the photo.

My grandparents laughed nervously. I wondered if that was because they weren't used to being photographed, or because they didn't believe in ghosts. No-one in Perth seemed to believe in any kind of ghost, except, perhaps, my father. And my mother, who seemed haunted less by ghosts in our Australian life, than by shadowy apprehensions of her own and others' unspeakable pain.

※

My father's photo of the extended family in Perth

My grandparents seated in their deckchairs, flanked on one side by Aunty Mercedes and on the other by my mother and myself. Aunty Mercedes dips her head slightly towards them, dark hair neatly bobbed, spectacles glinting in the sun.

My grandmother, dressed in her best pastel frock and white leather court shoes, has just lowered her hand after fussing with her hair. Her teeth and smile are small, as befits a lady.

The rest of us have wide smiles with large teeth. Except my mother, who is not smiling at all.

In the background, my grandparents' well-kept garden is totally cleared of native bush, with just a birdbath surrounded by rosebushes and lawn. It appears there is nothing to hide there, and nowhere to hide.

NOT A REAL WAR

A NEW neighbour shifted into the State Housing Commission house next door. A wild-eyed young man with crew-cut hair and moustache, chain-smoking on his front verandah and often wearing sunglasses as he surveyed the street. I was afraid of him.

'Don't worry. I've talked to him. His name's Michael. He looks like that because he's only recently come back from fighting in the Vietnam War,' my mother reassured me as she watered the yellow Peace roses in our front garden. 'He wears sunglasses a lot because bomb blast flashes hurt his eyes. Now they're sensitive to light.'

I kept my ears peeled for more clues about him. My mother left our bedroom windows open on hot summer nights to catch the sea breeze. Mine overlooked Michael's; through his sheer nylon curtain I could see a wardrobe and the foot of his bed. Sometimes in the middle of the night, I heard thumping sounds. Like footsteps on wooden floorboards, only louder.

Sometimes fast and staccato, sometimes so slow and irregular I thought they had finished, until the next flurry of thumps.

What was he doing? His light was always off when the noise happened. It must've been something he wanted kept secret. I lay awake listening, until the thumping stopped after five or ten minutes. Sometimes, straight after it stopped, I'd see his bedroom light come on, then turn off again within a minute.

When I told my mother one breakfast about the sounds, she looked puzzled for only a moment.

'Ah. Michael told me he has bad dreams.'

'What kind of bad dreams?'

'About being in the war.'

'What *kind* of dreams about being in the war?'

'About ... looking for one of his army mates after he ... disappeared in Vietnam.'

'How did he disappear?'

'Well. A bomb blew up when Michael and his mate were walking near the jungle at night.'

'And what happened to him?'

'I'm not sure.' I knew she was lying. 'But I think his mate died. Michael dreams he's on his knees searching for his friend. When he wakes, he's actually on his knees searching through the bottom of his wardrobe, throwing his shoes from there onto the floor. That's probably what those noises are that you hear at night. Isn't that sad?'

'I don't know,' I replied, wishing my mother would tell

me the kinds of things I wanted to know. 'Just sounds weird to me.'

'Remember that when people seem weird, it's usually caused by something,' she said.

'Can I have milk and sugar on rice instead of curry tonight?' I asked.

※

While my mother was at the supermarket one afternoon, my school friend Jan and I saw Michael sitting on his verandah smoking, watching us play on the lawn between the jarrah trees and the Peace roses.

'My mum thinks your new next-door neighbour's nuts,' Jan whispered to me as we changed our Barbie dolls out of their mini-skirted nurse's uniforms and into ball gowns.

'He just got back from fighting in Vietnam. Dad says it's another Asian war.'

'When was the other one?'

'In Singapore when my dad was a kid.'

'Oh yeah. My dad says that's why your dad's so skinny.'

'He is not.'

'Is so. Mum and Dad reckon the Australian and American soldiers who fought in Vietnam are murderers, even though they were fighting for the good Asians. They killed ladies and babies and kids as well as the bad Asians.'

'Is that true?'

'Mum said he's a creep. She says there were probably

other bad things the soldiers in Vietnam did. The newspaper says so. She said to stay away from him.' She looked at the blue shorts I wore. 'Those aren't really hot-pants. Too long. My shorts are real hot-pants. They're all the rage now.'

'Don't care.' But I preferred her bright pink shorts.

'And my Barbie's clothes are all the rage too.'

Jan's blonde Barbie wore a low-cut red ball dress and stilettos; my Barbie wore a more sedate green. Both the colours of good luck for my old Chinese neighbours in Singapore.

'He's still looking at us.'

'Sshh. Let's take the Barbies to the bush so he can't see us.'

'I'm not allowed to go to the bush without telling Mum.'

'It's okay to just go to the edge. We won't go deep where you can get lost. Or see the new Asian market gardens. Mum says they wee and poo on their gardens to make them grow. They spread disease. She said they're another kind of yellow peril.'

'What's a yellow peril?'

'Asians who have yellow skin. They get into Australia and they spread disease. Mum said your dad's not that kind of Asian. He's brown, not yellow. And he married your mum, so she probably taught him how to be clean.'

Suddenly the returned soldier stood up and came towards the low picket fence separating his front yard from ours. Jan and I glanced speechlessly at each other, grabbed our Barbies and ran down the street, crossing the busy intersection to the bush. He didn't seem to be following us. After we'd caught our breath, we sat under the she-oaks and made beds for the Barbies out of the fallen leaves. Each of them had lost a stiletto on the run.

'Doesn't matter. We'll look for them on the way home. Pretend they are going to get their beauty sleep before they go to the ball,' said Jan, 'after a hard day nursing.' But a shadow fell over us after we'd bedded them down. The soldier. He'd followed us after all, and was standing closer to me than he'd ever been. He was wearing his sunglasses, so even close-up I couldn't see if he was crazy or not.

'You shouldn't come here,' he warned in a gravelly voice. 'There might be poisonous snakes. Hidden weapons, explosives.'

We picked up our ball-gowned Barbies, wielding them like talismans in front of us as we ran all the way home, forgetting all about their lost shoes.

✳

'Jan says her mum says our new neighbour is nuts,' I said to my mother as I heaped four tablespoonsful of Milo into half a glass of milk.

'You mean Michael? I don't think he's dangerous.'

'How do you know?'

'I can tell sad crazy people from dangerous crazy people.'

'How can you tell?'

'Ohh ... because I'm a bit mad myself.' She looked down

sombrely at her hands for just a moment before smiling at me. 'Go look in the bathroom mirror. You look a bit mad too. More Milo on your face than in your stomach.'

I stood in front of the bathroom mirror until I'd wiped every bit of my Milo moustache off. It was the first time my mother had said what I had thought: that something wasn't quite right about her.

※

Photos of my mother's face at thirty

In the black and white photographs my father took of my mother a few weeks after Aunty Mercedes left, she is looking into the distance, rather than at the camera. She does not smile. Her dark eyes look wistful, her lips full but sensitive. She wears her hair back in a bun, revealing the mole at the outer corner of her jaw. The one the Chinese fortune teller in Singapore had said predestined her to keep her troubles and 'unspeakable pain' to herself; the one that's concealed when she lets her hair down.

Far from Home

ABOUT a year later, a doctor removed the mole from my mother's jaw, and she began seeing a psychologist once a fortnight. She caught a bus to the psychologist every Wednesday, because she'd never learned to drive.

'What's a psy-*chologist*?' I asked her, stumbling over the long word as she picked sprigs of rosemary. *Rosemary for remembrance*, she'd told me several times. 'Oh, just someone to talk to about things,' she replied, but her nonchalant manner didn't match her words or her face, and her hands smelled more strongly of cigarettes than rosemary.

※

Between selling his second-hand black Austin and waiting to pick up his new white Valiant Safari station wagon, my father caught the bus to and from work. One evening, he returned home shaking. He sat at the table, head in his hands.

'Ah yah!'

'What's wrong, my Love?' Mum asked.

'Some youths at the bus stop called me a poxy slope. Told me to take my diseases and slanty eyes back to where I came from.'

'But you don't have slanty eyes. What's a poxy slope?' I asked.

'A name no person should ever be called.' Mum served Dad a huge plateful of roast chicken and vegetables, everything except the sweet potato. She never served him sweet potato. It was too much like the yams he'd had to eat when his family lived in the Malay jungle during the war.

My father ate his dinner even faster than usual, as if fortifying himself against future catastrophe. I ate my chicken and stuffing but left all the roast vegetables and peas on my plate.

'Eat all your dinner,' he said.

'I don't like it all.'

'Ah yah! Eat everything on your plate! In the war we dug our own yams from the ground and went to bed starving every night.'

'Eat some vegetables, then you can have some ice-cream,' my mother coaxed me, serving Dad a large bowl of ice-cream with Milo heaped on top. 'You won't have to go to the bus stop when the new car comes, Love.'

'*Saudade*,' he said, before shovelling the ice-cream into his mouth.

'What's *saudade*?' I asked.

'A Portuguese word for missing or longing for someone or some place. Daddy's missing home. Singapore.'

'But this is our home. Isn't it?'

※

In the months following that night, I had nightmares about running through the streets of our suburb with my father, trying with my broad Australian accent and sunburned skin to convince unknown neighbours not to throw their broken beer bottles and barbecue briquettes at him from behind their

fences. Our skin already burning, with something other than
fire.

※

I choose a female kitten from a stray cat's litter on the bush
block. The mother has abandoned them, so the neighbours are
trying to find homes for the three kittens.

'Why do you like that one?' my mother asks me.

'She's black and white and every shade of brown,' I say.
'What's that called?'

'She's a tortoiseshell cat,' says my mother. 'Piebald.'

'Eurasian,' grins my father.

'I'll call her Sweety-Pie. Why did the mother leave?' I ask.

Mum crosses her arms, pinches the skin just above her
elbow. 'Some mothers aren't happy being mothers, I suppose,'
she says, looking towards the horizon.

※

My father's Australian citizenship certificate arrived in the
post. He turned the certificate over, read the words on the
back out loud:

'"Francis Xavier Oliveira. Nationality and or citizenship
(prior to grant of this certificate): Citizen of Malaysia. Colour
of eyes: Brown. Colour of Hair: Black. Visible distinguishing
marks: Nil." They didn't mention I look Asian. Or my skin
colour,' he concluded, satisfied. My mother's smile brimmed
with relief as she served each of us Peter's ice-cream drizzled

98

with Marsala liquor, Dad's favourite.

After dessert, my father wiped his hands carefully and held up the certificate so we could see the cameo portrait of Queen Elizabeth the Second at the top, with pale pink skin and rouged cheeks, wearing a yellow gown and a corsage of yellow wattle beneath her diamond tiara and necklace.

This portrait of the queen reminded me of Queenie, the canary we'd left behind in Singapore. I imagined her swinging in her wicker cage on my uncle and aunty's apartment balcony in the South China Sea breeze, singing her songs of love and warning.

'Yellow's the colour royalty wore in Malaya too,' my father said. 'One of your Eurasian great-grandmothers had royal connections there. She received a stipend from the Malay royal family until the war.'

'So maybe I really am a princess!'

'No, that great-grandmother was just a lady-in-waiting.'

'Am I a lady-in-waiting too?'

'Maybe we both are,' my mother smiled wistfully.

'Can I have a yellow dress for my birthday, Mum?'

'I'll try my best.'

'And a canary, Dad?'

'Our backyard has room for a whole aviary full of canaries, and my English colleague offered me some the other day,' he replied. 'Notice this certificate's signed by Hubert Opperman? He's not only the State Minister for Immigration. He's an Australian Olympic cycling champion.'

＊

That weekend, my father enclosed the back wall of the old wooden toolshed with flyscreen wire and painted it Western Australian Public Works Department green, from a leftover tin of paint he'd found at one of the dams he'd worked on. He installed empty plastic Wescobee honey containers as nests.

On Sunday, he rose early and drove to fetch nine canaries from his English colleague: one red factor, three golden rollers, two crested, and three lizard canaries. Perhaps they too sang songs of love and warning, but with so many of them singing at once, it was difficult to be sure. I named one of the crested canaries Queen Elizabeth the Second, but mostly called her Queenie, after the canary we'd left behind in Singapore.

Sweety-Pie the cat sat every day staring into the cage, licking her lips, biding her time.

＊

It was my job to feed the canaries. Over the next year, I watched Queenie's pink hatchlings emerge from eggs, saw maggots a few weeks later in the bodies of those who didn't survive, watched her fledglings spread their wings.

In a careless moment one morning, I held the aviary door open too long and Queenie escaped. I ran back to the house, worried my father would be angry at me. I dared not tell him.

But standing at the kitchen window as my mother plaited my hair after dad left for work, I saw Queenie fly from a banksia branch into the bright blue summer sky, a Qantas jet high above her, both of them heading northwards, maybe towards Singapore.

'Queenie!' I shouted, my plait unravelling as I ran from my startled mother.

By the time I reached the back door, Queenie had disappeared.

Scanning the sky and the street trees for the canary, I ran all the way to the edge of the bush where the returned soldier had warned us about bombs. I looked up into the branches of the towering jarrah eucalyptus trees for Queenie, but dared not go further. For that was where the jungle-like bush replaced our suburb, with all its hidden perils. Better to turn my back on it all, run home. But wait – what was that flash of yellow and faint chirping to the north? It sounded like the song of a small creature far from home, her call of freedom overwhelmed by distance, receding towards Asia and infinity.

※

Other unphotographed historic moments at home

Watching the first man walking on the moon on our first television, as we mop up Dad's kofta curry with some sliced Wonder White bread.

My aproned mother, her hair in a slightly flattened beehive style, serving slices of my house-shaped birthday cake to me, royalty in my new yellow dress.

My mother telling my father with relief when he returned home from work, that she'd heard on the radio the Labor Party wanted to remove the White Australia Policy.

'But will that make any difference to the way people like me are treated in these suburbs every day?' he asks. My mother thoughtful but unable to answer, her hands trembling as she places a plate of Australian beef steak on the table before him.

'It's tough,' she tells him, 'but it's cooked with love.'

EMPTY NESTS

WHEN he worked for the Metropolitan Water Board, my father often took us to dams and rivers for picnics on the weekend. The food gradually changed from a pot of home-cooked curry to chops and sausages fried on greasy public barbecues and wrapped in Tip Top bread with Rosella tomato sauce, but there was always a thermos of Bushells tea and a tin of Family Assorted biscuits. After he'd eaten, my father would inspect the dam gauges and water quality before taking me for swimming lessons at a nearby stretch of river. All my life, my mother was afraid of drowning, and that I might drown too.

'Don't go too deep!' Mum would shout from the banks, pacing up and down watching us, until we emerged safely.

✳

Sometimes in summer, my father takes me to swim at the beach half an hour's drive away from home. Mum doesn't go to the beach with us often, because her pale skin burns easily. And because she's afraid of being drowned by big waves or rips.

'Don't take her too deep,' she warns him. 'Stay right next to her.'

My father takes me to Port Beach, over the road from the huge Ampol petrol storage tanks. Sometimes we see passenger liners and cargo ships heading out to sea or being ushered by tugboats into the harbour.

'That's where I arrived from Singapore when I studied at university,' he says. 'This is the Indian Ocean. It meets the South China Sea at the islands below Singapore.'

While he's busy practising his Australian crawl just beyond the break-line, a huge wave rises too close to me. I don't know how to dive under it, and am too frightened to swim over the top. It looms over me, sucks me into the depths where I tumble and lose my breath, before rising to gasp just once before the backwash pushes me further out of my depth. A Peter's twin-pole wrapper floats past in a net of sunlight as the gritty floor of the ocean scrapes my back; I glimpse the net of sunlight sucked up by the darker deep just before I begin gulping salt water. An image of Aunty Mercedes waving at me from the airport terminal recedes quickly before my vision turns black. Then I feel someone lift my head back to the surface.

'Don't tell Mum,' Dad says as he drags me gasping, to the shore.

※

'Where does the Indian Ocean really end?' I ask Mum the next day as I draw patterns on the edges of her shopping list. 'Dad told me it begins below Port Beach and ends just before Singapore.'

'Well. That's one way of looking at it.'

'What d'you mean?'

One of her considered silences. I read the shopping list as I wait.

Chook pellets
Peanut paste
Weet-Bix
Nescafé
Bex
Sobranies

Sobranies? Isn't that the name of those cigarettes in bright colours she smokes on special occasions with friends? Nearly the same colours as the maths counting rods at school. But Bex? What is Bex?

'Well,' she finally replies to my earlier question. 'The Indian Ocean merges with the Great Southern Ocean and the South China and Timor Seas. With the Swan River and all the other big Western Australian rivers. And goes all the way to the east African coast and joins the rivers there. So another way of looking at it might be that there is no end to most oceans. They just merge with other bodies of water.'

'Phew. That makes my brain overflow,' I say, drawing a line at the bottom of her shopping list.

✳

All the canaries' nests in the plastic Wescobee honey pots empty over the next few years as the birds escape or die in the aviary, one by one, of maternal neglect, raiding by rats, unknown Australian diseases or old age.

'That's strange. I can't hear any canaries singing,' my mother said.

'The last canary has died,' I admitted. 'I found her dead this morning.'

'Don't blame yourself,' my mother consoled. 'All creatures die or fly away, sooner or later. We all lose things we love.' She turned away just a second too late to hide her tears from me.

I hugged her but felt nowhere near wise enough to understand why she was so sad.

✳

On some autumn weekends of my ninth year, the sun hidden by clouds, our neighbourhood quiet apart from the melancholy farewell of magpies, I felt the loneliness of not belonging.

'What's wrong?' Mum asked.

'I feel sad and bored.'

'Ask Jan over to play?'

'Jan's too busy with other friends to play with me.'

'Come with me to the garden while I pick some herbs.'

I trailed reluctantly behind her, passing the empty aviary, the aging chooks roosting in the wattle tree, the rusty old swing.

'Look!' she said. 'When you're sad, try looking around with your eyes open wide.'

'At what?'

'Look at the passing of these beautiful days. See the way the sky shifts. The changes in light on the leaves. Birds and people on their way to other places. Each moment is unique. Remember them. But don't be afraid to forget, either.' She paused. 'Those clouds with the sun's rays spreading from behind them. Cirrus, nimbus, cumulus. Some people call those gold-edged sunrays God rays.'

'Why?'

'Maybe because they think they're shining from heaven? They're clearest in the late afternoon when a storm's brewing.'

'Do you believe in God?'

'I don't know.'

'What is God?'

'I guess I'm not really sure what God is.' She looked wistfully away from the sky, as if she doubted she'd find the answer there. Then she summonsed a smile and looked at me as magpies caroled in the distance. 'Listen. You can almost hear the happiness of the days ahead.'

My mother, trying to teach me how to deal with loss, how to find happiness in a given moment, how to read the clouds; yet unable to help her own sadness.

※

She was invited by Jan's mother to join a book club run by women who mostly lived in the more affluent part of our suburb, closer to the river.

'A chance for me to reconnect with my love of literature and make new friends,' I heard her say to Dad.

When it was her turn to host the book club, she used the birthday money her parents had given her to buy a coffee percolator, freshly ground Italian coffee and a printed cotton Indian dress that fastened at the neckline with tiny bells.

'Hmm, Jan's mother. Think I'll work late at the office tomorrow night,' Dad grumbled.

'She's just … ignorant,' my mother said. 'You're probably the first Asian she's seen.'

'Huh.' He retreated to his recliner in front of the television, turned up loud his white-suited, dark-skinned countryman Kamahl singing 'Sounds of Goodbye' on the ABC.

※

The next day my mother baked a chocolate and nutmeg cake dark and earthy in texture. She wound her waist-length hair into a loose bun and wore her best sandals and her new Indian dress.

The other women arrived early in the evening, wearing Mary Quant frocks or silk robes, teetering in high heels that made their long necklaces and earrings swing. They walked past our kitchen trailing perfume and laughter, their blonde hair artfully styled. A few of them glanced uncomprehendingly at the toomba-toomba on the benchtop, traces of last night's curry spices and lemongrass still in its bowl. One of them sniffed the air apprehensively, as if she'd caught a whiff of something dangerous and unknown.

Sent to bed soon after the women arrived, I went to the toilet often, eavesdropping, hoping to hear them talk about *Fear of Flying*, their book of the month. I'd read the word sex on the back cover of Mum's copy, hoped to overhear from the women a revelation or two. I smelled their cigarette smoke mingled with their expensive perfume, glimpsed brightly coloured Sobranie cigarettes between their manicured fingers.

But the women talked about facials, boutique shopping or home renovations. My mother, who had none of these things in her daily life, remained mostly silent. Until one of the other women said in her British accent, 'Now, talking about our book. I'd like a zipless fuck,' and I heard my mother laugh, but more quietly than the others.

*

When Dad received a small pay rise, he drove us in the Valiant Safari to look at homes in the newer southern suburbs. Passing streets of old pastel-painted fibro State Housing Commission houses, he'd stopped once outside a display home in a new suburb across the road from a swamp, giving them a dazzling view of the sun setting over the drought-stricken paperbark trees.

'What swamp is that?' Dad asked the navy blue-blazered real estate agent carefully wiping dog-shit off his white leather shoes onto the lawn.

'It's a *lake,* not a swamp,' the agent insisted. 'Where do you come from?'

'Singapore.'

'Ah. Not many lakes there. This is a million-dollar view.' I saw his mouthful of gold fillings when he smiled at me and winked, wondered if they were supposed to match the gold medallion hanging on the chain around his neck. 'She your daughter?'

'Yes.'

'Much paler than you.'

'My wife over there on the verandah has English parents,' Dad said, appearing to shrug the agent's comments off.

Mum glanced suspiciously at the agent, took a deep breath as if she were readying herself to retort to him, but exhaled a long breath instead and took my hand, leading me inside after the two men.

Dad was unsettled by the exposed brick wall in the lounge-room.

'Shouldn't it be plastered white like the others?'

'It's a feature wall,' the real estate agent explained. 'It's very fashionable now to have exposed brick feature walls in the living areas.' To contrast with the whiteness? 'You'll love the brick barbecue in the courtyard too.' He pushed the glass sliding doors open. 'Brand new Flexalum patio.'

We walked out to the brick barbecue. Dad ran his finger along the barbecue plate and murmured to Mum: 'We could use it for satay. Or steak and sausages.'

'Now you're getting the hang of it,' said the agent. 'I must say you speak perfect English.'

'My family listened to the BBC on the radio every day in Singapore,' Dad said. 'We were all British subjects.'

※

Over the next few years, we spent many weekends visiting suburban display homes and reading the new homes articles in the newspapers. In the early- to mid-1970s, we saw display homes evolve from squat red or blond brick boxes with low-ceilinged living areas and sliding glass rear doors opening onto Flexalum-covered patios. The new designs had open-plan living areas with soaring exposed beams, pergolas and external brick colours which were as varied as Arnott's Family Assorted biscuits.

We visited houses of clinker brick, or rendered in terracotta colours, or white-washed, or built from stone. Some of their kitchens mimicked rustic European village houses. Some of them had high-walled courtyards mimicking Spanish or Mexican haciendas. Some of them had lofty ceilings mimicking cathedrals, but none of them appeared influenced by Asia.

My father liked a modest two-bedroom house with an external arched verandah and carport.

'A Spanish influence,' a real estate agent explained. 'I can see you're a cosmopolitan family.'

'Too kitsch,' my mother murmured to my father, 'and all that white paint to maintain.'

After the real estate agent left, she suggested, 'Let's go for a block closer to the river and a more contemporary, larger house design to harmonise with that.'

'How do you think we can afford that?'

'I could try and get a job.'

'No wife of mine will go out to work,' he said adamantly. My mother looked disappointed, but did not reply.

They were still drawn to calm bodies of water, both of them. But those few years of dreaming of a new home to share might have been the last time my parents dreamed together.

※

When I was about to begin high school, Dad received a promotion and another pay rise. My parents finally decided to buy a block with big trees on the other side of the swamp and build a split-level project house with exposed beams and high ceilings. They chose dark clinker bricks and pale mortar that resembled Hydro Creams, my father's favourite chocolate biscuits.

'It will have three bedrooms, two bathrooms and three toilets,' he told Grandpa and Grandma.

'Why do you need three toilets?' my grandmother asked.

'One for each floor,' he replied.

＊

We visited the building site a few times a week, standing in the gradually rising rooms to imagine how we would furnish and live in them. Maybe a tan leather lounge suite to replace the old green vinyl one the cat had clawed holes in; and a jarrah wooden dining table and matching chairs to continue the new block's Australian bush theme inside.

But the hidden costs in the new house increased so much we couldn't afford new furniture. My parents settled for the cheapest floor coverings for every room except the cathedral-ceilinged lounge-room, master bedroom and staircase, which would be carpeted in pure wool beige shag pile. Just straw Honan squares for the small bedroom, study and passage, cheap Chinese quarry tiles for the kitchen and dining room.

'Just like our apartment floorings in Singapore,' Dad said.

But my mother stood in the open-plan living room and shivered, even though the summer heat beat down outside and all the external doors and windows were closed. She said she could feel a cold wind blowing through, unlike any she'd felt before.

＊

My father will not build another aviary in our new backyard. Instead he builds a new pergola at the rear of the house and paints it Mission Brown, the same colour as the exposed beams in our kitchen and living areas.

Beneath this pergola one Saturday, he barbecues sticks of spiced satay he'd made to his mother's old recipe, handwritten on a yellowed page in the back of Mrs Ellice Handy's *My Favourite Recipes*. A special treat for Mum's old university friend Dianne, recently returned from Europe with her French husband, Philippe.

'Such exotic food! Nice house too. Quite avant-garde,' laughs Dianne, tapping her Schiaparelli pink French kitten-heel shoes against the brick paving as we finish the satay and rice cakes.

'Come upstairs to the cathedral-ceilinged mezzanine living room,' my father replies enthusiastically. 'From there you can see the new shopping mall. It has a Chinese restaurant and a range of international foods in the supermarket.'

I eavesdrop on Dianne and Philippe talking about open marriages in the open-plan living room.

'Bhagwan says open marriages and free love are liberating. Europe and America have had them for years. Perth people are way too provincial. They need to broaden their horizons with Eastern and European philosophies,' Dianne tells my father as she hitches up her silk skirt, revealing her black lace slip.

'You should come to our *Group*,' says Philippe, as if emphasising its importance.

'Add a bit of spice to it,' Dianne agrees, winking at my father and smoothing her skirt over her hips with her hands while my mother painstakingly prepares dessert and percolates coffee in the kitchen.

※

The only things we had taken from our old garden were potted plants and cuttings: lavender and geraniums originally transplanted from my grandparents' garden; my mother's herbs, the lemongrass and the lemon tree in the Shanghai pot from Singapore. Perth was in the grip of a drought, so my parents had planted native plants in our new garden. As she watered them carefully, my mother addressed them all as if she was introducing good friends or family.

'Eucalyptus caesia, melaleuca quinquenervia, grevillea, coastal moort. Hovea, or Weeping Wanderer,' she intoned gently, as if talking to them like this would encourage them to put down roots and reach their full potential in unfamiliar soil. The same way she'd talked to me in our first Perth house. She still talked to me like that, but less often. It was as if the distances between us in the new house were too big to easily bridge, and she'd become preoccupied with her own survival since Dianne and Philippe had entered her life.

※

After taking a few snapshots of Dianne and Philippe when they visited, Dad stopped taking photographs as frequently.

He didn't turn either of the new bathrooms into a darkroom for developing photos on weekends. But the new native shrubs grew beneath the lofty jarrah trees, and willy-wagtails nested the following year in the coastal moort planted near the kitchen window, after courting all through the night. And some bush bees shifted from the jarrah trees into an unsealed cavity between my bedroom ceiling and the upstairs balcony. Their honey dripped on my adolescent acne, like some kind of blessing as I lay in bed.

※

By my mid-teens, my father had lost interest in taking family photos altogether. He stored his Rolleiflex twin-lens and Box Brownie cameras at the back of his wardrobe, but let me borrow the Pentax automatic single-lens reflex camera a work colleague had recently sold to him cheap. I read its instruction manual and taught myself how to focus, how to read the flickering needle of the built-in light meter and the light of fleeting moments across faces and landscapes.

In high school photography classes, I learned how to adjust aperture stops and shutter speeds to give more or less depth of field. When to use natural light, and when to use a flashbulb. In the school darkroom, I learned in the glow of the red light how to avoid the groping boys, how to wind the undeveloped snapshots from the film cartridge into the cylindrical black developing tank, bathing the film in three solutions to turn it into a transparent strip of negative images. Developer, stop bath, fixer.

After the negatives dried and the groping boys had gone home, I practised in the darkroom the slow magic of making positive prints from the negatives: sliding them carefully into the enlarging lamp's negative carrier, slipping a piece of photographic paper on the flat surface of the enlarger's base and timing the enlarger's light through a negative to fall on the paper's chemical-infused emulsion.

And bathing the paper in four trays of solution:

The developer, smelling like a blend of ammonia and tamarind paste. Watching the details of a passing person or incident coalesce like fetal cells in fast-motion on the paper's surface beneath the watery solution, re-emerging as a still image.

The stop-bath that halted the darkening; then the fixer and finally the hypo-clearer to give the image a long life.

Scrutinising those newborn images in daylight for the details in their darkest depths, brightest highlights and every shade in between. And for the joy of recalling moving people and moments that might otherwise be forgotten.

※

Portrait of my parents

The only photo I take during my adolescence of my mother and father standing together. Together, but not.

My father slightly blurred, as if already moving away, looking at something beyond the frame. My mother quite still, eyes lowered, as if looking inward at something only she could see.

PHOTOSENSITIVITIES
AND NOCTURNES

MY mother developed a stronger aversion to bright sunlight that summer, and needed her own kind of darkroom.

'Photosensitivity,' the doctor told her when he saw the rash on her pale skin. The migraines she suffered grew more frequent and severe, forcing her to draw her bedroom curtains and lie down for hours.

I guessed the migraines now were mostly caused by the heat, glare and her photosensitivity. She preferred the night, often staying awake past midnight, opening the windows to catch the sea breeze. Sometimes on my way back from the toilet to my bedroom after midnight, I heard the crackling of dust and scratches amplified by Dad's Her Majesty's Voice speakers as Mum lowered his record-player needle over the teak-boxed turntable from Singapore. Increasingly, she listened to my father's old classical records in the parapet-walled living room as his absences at night grew longer and more frequent, and summer passed into autumn.

※

One night before bed, I ask my mother what music she likes best.

'Mozart and Debussy and Chopin. I like Chopin's nocturnes a lot,' she replies.

'What's a nocturne?'

'A musical composition evocative of the night. In the Middle Ages, the term nocturne was used to describe the night prayers said by monks in places like monasteries, between two hours after midnight and dawn.'

'So those old men were keeping their eyes on time when everyone else was asleep?'

She smiles but says nothing.

Later that night, I glimpse her sitting alone in the living room on my way back from the bathroom. Is she keeping an eye on the night? It's past midnight, but the streetlight shines through the window, illuminating her. Her face profile a half moon, almost glowing. She looks as if she is praying as the quiet music rises in waves, overcoming the static of dust and scratches on the record.

What is she praying for?

※

Over my middle years of high school, the times when we were all together as a family in one place dwindled. My father began staying out all night and eating dinner out, especially on weekends. My mother's careful cooking of dishes from Elizabeth David's books in the new kitchen diminished as his absences increased; her pink and green Marimekko apron lay scorched and abandoned at the bottom of the laundry basket.

Late one Saturday night, lying in my bedroom below theirs, I heard my mother crying and shouting. I knew my father hadn't yet come home. I stumbled up the dark stairs and turned on the light, to find her alone in bed, talking in her sleep.

'Help!' she shouted, but after that, her voice lowered so much I couldn't make sense of whatever else she said.

❋

The next morning, I told my mother about her shouting in her sleep. She hesitated before speaking.

'I've dreamed since I was a child about a man breaking into my room while I'm lying in bed. The room changes from dream to dream, but it often has louvred windows, like the verandah sleepouts had in some of the old wheatbelt houses we lived in then. I know this man will hurt me. In the dream, I am so frightened I don't know whether to keep quiet or to scream for help. But he holds me down before I can scream. When I finally try to scream, I lose my voice and I'm woken either by a total darkness which finishes the dream, or by a terrible pain in my head.'

'A headache?'

'My migraines often start straight after the nightmare,' she said.

※

When my father returns home late one morning after spending the whole Friday night out, I overhear their conversation.

'Where have you been all night? I stay awake worrying.'

'Ah yah!' he shouts, 'I go to Dianne and Philippe's Group.' He storms towards the front door again. 'No wonder I don't come back at night. You carry on endlessly! Even in your sleep!'

※

Later that day, Dianne rings and speaks to Mum. I hear my mother put down the phone, enter the bathroom, turn on the shower and sob quietly. Is she hoping the shower might drown out her weeping?

'What's wrong?' I ask when she comes out of the bathroom about half an hour later, dabbing a towel to her eyes.

'My eyes are just watery,' she replies. 'Did you know about seventy-three percent of the human heart and brain are water? Even bones are watery. Thirty-one percent. Water acts as a shock absorber in our bodies.'

'Is that why you drink so many cups of tea and coffee?'

'They're just to help me keep going.'

※

In my third year of high school I made friends with Lucy, who lived near the beach and had the blonde-streaked hair and suntan to prove it. But Lucy had already started going out with boys and smirked patronisingly when I confided in her my interest in a quiet boy with wild sun-bleached hair named David, who was in our art class. David and I were both too shy to talk to each other during a whole term of art classes, the only classes we had in common. Lucy appraised his hair and tanned skin.

'Looks like he surfs,' she said. 'He's sort of cool.'

The following Monday was cold and rainy. Just before lunch, Lucy said casually as she looked over my shoulder: 'Saw David on the weekend at the beach. Pashed with him. Going out with him next weekend.'

The lunch bell rang. Shivering, I grabbed my bag and ran all the way home to confide in my mother what Lucy had just told me.

'So, whose problem is that, do you think?' she asked me gently as I gulped the expertly percolated coffee with cream she'd made me. She was still in her dressing-gown. When it fell open as she made me a sandwich, the bleak grey light coming through the kitchen window revealed how thin she'd become. She piled the sandwich high and put an extra dollop of cream in my coffee.

'Don't know,' I muttered. My mother remained silent. I rubbed my pimply chin and wished for more advice from her. But it was one of her empathic, considered silences, and I sat bathing in it and drinking more coffee for a few minutes until I felt warm again, and strong enough to go back to school and face those unpredictable people who might or might not be my friends.

And I see, years later, that she wanted me to find my own answers to those kinds of questions, which I understand now were questions she had too.

※

Woken by an unearthly howl just before dawn a few Sundays later, I wonder at first if my mother is having a nightmare. But the howl is too high-pitched, and it seems to come from outside. The garage light flickers on. I open the front door to find my father standing at the rear of his car, looking down at a dark mess on the ground.

I walk towards him, smell wine and confusion on his breath. He's just driven too fast up the driveway. The dark mess he looks at is Sweety-Pie. She is silent, unbreathing, her lower body mangled and bloody.

'Go back to bed,' my father mutters to me, grabbing the spade.

From my bed, I hear him digging a hole in the garden. I lie listening to the damp earth falling, and the first birds singing the cat into the ground.

My mother became even thinner. Once after she fainted, she told me she'd sometimes wondered as she regained consciousness, *Who am I? Neither Elspeth Green, nor Mrs Elspeth Oliveira. Just an infant who has not learned how to speak or run, unable to escape.* Her comments and the expression on her face had seemed childlike to me, not what a mother should say.

※

After my father left for work one morning, I noticed bruises on either side of my mother's neck, the size and span of adult fingertips.

'Where did those bruises come from?' I asked through my sleepy stupor. She shrugged and pulled her dressing gown collar up.

'Eat your breakfast. Don't be late for school.' She paused. 'It's important you get a good education and a good job, Sally Jones. Don't depend on a man to support you.'

※

Some evenings as I half-heartedly attempted homework, I imagined I heard the ghost of the cat pacing upstairs. But it was really the ghost of happier times, and Mum. Both of them waiting for release.

Dust motes rose from the living room curtains as we parted them early evenings to look out across the swamp to the car lights rushing along the highway. The months of our unhappiness lengthened into seasons, seasons lengthened into another year. Each setting sun revealing the dust deepening on the windowsills of my parents' dream home.

※

I grew into a gangly seventeen-year-old, stretching my wings and staying out late with schoolfriends some weekend nights, readying myself to fly from the nest forever. But not as late as my father, who often didn't come home until late Sunday morning after going out on Friday night.

Mum wandered around the edges of the drought-stricken paperbark swamp nearby, or around the shopping mall at sale times, buying romantic clothes at bargain prices. A flowing red velvet dress, a silk kaftan, a tapestry-print midi skirt, a white linen peasant blouse, a black coat with a high faux-fur collar and cuffs. But she had no suitor or event for which to wear them.

※

A few weeks before my final university entrance exams, I am surprised that Mum isn't standing by the kettle sipping her morning cup of tea as usual. It's already nine o'clock, and I'd heard Dad leave for work at eight. I go upstairs to her room, to find her still in bed, her face and neck strangely swollen.

'Mum! What's wrong?'

She simply shakes her head, just once, listlessly. Alarmed, I run downstairs and ring for a doctor.

❋

The doctor comes downstairs and speaks to me after examining Mum.

'She has blood poisoning. We need to get her to hospital straight away.' He lowers his voice. 'Has she suffered from depression recently?'

I don't know where to begin telling him, or whether I should begin at all.

❋

Discharged from hospital about a fortnight later, for weeks my mother rose late in the mornings, standing in her dressing-gown by the kettle. She often turned her back on me when I came into the room, spoke to me curtly or not at all. It seemed I'd done something wrong, but I didn't know what. I closed my bedroom door on my silent mother and absent father and tried to cram a year's worth of study into a week. I would get through my exams as best I could.

❋

When all the exams were finally over, I met my friends most days at the beach.

One morning as I grabbed my beach bag, Mum, still in her dressing-gown, stood by the kettle and murmured, 'I'm sorry I haven't been good to you lately. I was angry because I wanted to die, and you stopped that from happening when you called the doctor.' Steam rose from the kettle's spout but it spluttered instead of whistling.

'That's okay,' I said. But I didn't feel okay, not as I ran to catch the bus, not as I rode it all the way down Canning Highway and caught the train at Fremantle to the beach, not as I joined my friends on the white sand, not when I dived into the sunlit sea to try to clear my thoughts. I'd swum a lap of Leighton beach but, panic-stricken by thoughts about what my mother might do to herself while I was out, I barely heard my chattering schoolfriends. I could concentrate only on my silent hope that surely now, my mother wanted to live.

※

Some images I tried to forget

The blue bruises the size of a man's fingertips around my mother's neck.

The father-shaped gap at our dinner table most nights over the following months.

My mother's face and neck, swollen and pale against the pillow as she lies in bed, her eyes averted, not answering my questions about this.

The anger inflaming my father's face when I tell him that afternoon that the doctor has admitted Mum to hospital.

Aloneness

OVER-EXPOSURES

MY mother emerged gracious but damaged from the divorce. Her lawyer wanted to take my father 'to the cleaners', but my mother refused to fight my father's demands for more than his fair share of their assets. She still loved him, she told me, and thought he'd suffered enough hardship as he grew up during the war and its aftermath.

※

As we shared my eighteenth birthday lunch at the café overlooking the sea, my mother gave me a card showing a bird in flight. Inside, her usually small handwriting was larger and rounder than usual, as if she was making an effort to blossom and open:

> *How lucky I am to be your mother. I've watched you grow into such a thoroughly lovely person that I feel shy about saying too much. I wish (I've always wished this)*

that you could catch a glimpse of all that you reflect
for me, of a world beyond the reach of most, shown in
your ways of being kind, and seeking to understand, not
sparing the effort.

My love, and wishing you many more horizons of
happiness.

At the time, I read it not only as a carefully worded message of something to live up to; but as a reflection of the mother I had almost lost. I blinked my tears away before she could see them and slid the card inside the deep magenta leather-bound journal she'd given me as a gift.

'I hope I haven't passed on too many ghosts to you,' she said, taking my hand after lunch as we walked on the winter-cooled sand, our eyes on the grey clouds which were darkening where the sea met the sky.

※

My father's new wife, a middle-aged nurse named Trudi whom he'd met at Dianne's and Philippe's Group encounters, knew how to manage critical incidents and how to take the pulse of the times as well as people. She persuaded my mother to shift out of the house.

Trudi and Dad moved into our Hydro Cream brick family home the day we shifted out, their new king-sized bed coming first, wide as a stage. My mother and I followed the removalist's truck carrying her few worldly possessions, including the double bed she'd shared for so many years with my father, all the way to her new home.

The divorce settlement had given Mum just enough money to buy a 1960s one-bedroom flat up three flights of stairs, wedged between busy roads near the Perth CBD and Hyde Park, where she'd walked sometimes before she'd met my father. Was she trying to go back to her life before she met him, when other futures had been possible?

※

My mother found her crisp new Social Security's card in her new letterbox.

'See what I've become,' she told me, holding out her card for me to read:

PENSIONER. B CLASS WIDOW.

※

I shifted into a share house with a few students I met at university. The offspring of unhappily married or divorced parents, we were already experienced at surviving financially without much help from our parents. And to ducking and weaving around others to avoid conflict.

※

More efficient than my mother, Trudi installed a spa and replaced with paving much of the garden my parents had planted. Within weeks of shifting into our family home, she called the pest controllers to remove the bees and ants, a handyman to fix its cavities and cracks and a tree lopper to cut down the messy trees.

When I visited the first time months later, the bush bees whose hive had dripped honey on me as I lay on my bed, murmured their condolences from the creamy blossoms in the high branches of the only surviving jarrah tree, no longer to bless my face with their honey. And the Weeping Wanderer had been pruned back so hard it no longer wandered or wept any flowers.

※

I studied fine arts, photography and English at university. Mostly, I took photos of people, practising on my friends and parents. I caught a taxi to the university photography studio to print photos for one of my assessments. The taxi driver had a cockney English accent and a back seat piled high with boxes of beer and Scotch. I sat next to him in the front passenger seat, folded my arms tightly and glimpsed his florid double-chinned face and wide girth from the corner of my eye. He lit a cigarette from his packet of Dunhills, revved through the quiet streets leading to the studio. It was Chinese New Year, and his radio was tuned to a program interviewing a successful Perth Chinese businesswoman.

'Bloody Asians. They're taking over the country,' he said, shaking his head. 'Sooner do it with a woman with hairy legs than an Asian woman.'

I turned my face the other way and tried to tuck my legs out of sight. Part Asian and fully unshaven, but maybe the taxi driver hadn't noticed. Just keep quiet, I told myself, maybe he'll stop talking.

'They should all go back to where they came from,' he persisted. We'd arrived outside the photography studio, but I could no longer keep quiet.

'I am part Asian. Both you and I are just migrants here, you know,' I said over my shoulder as I disembarked. Outside the summer evening descended, bearing the smell of eucalyptus trees. I inhaled its scent as if it might save me.

※

The first roll of film I developed in the university darkroom included shots of my father and my mother in their separate homes. In the darkroom, I printed a proof-sheet of my snapshots of them, watching their complexions become too light or too dark in the developing solution. I'd either under- or over-exposed them at that split second that I tried to capture their true image. I held tight to the proof sheet – all of us together in one place.

※

When I showed my photography tutor the proof sheet just outside the darkroom door, he said:

'Hmm, the white lady's been given too much light and the Abo not enough.'

'He's Eurasian, actually.'

'What'd you say? He's Jewish?'

'*Eur-asian.*'

'Well, whether he's European or Asian, you've given him the wrong exposure.'

I swallowed my exasperation. 'What can I do to fix that?'

'With this kind of SLR camera, you have to take the lens right up to the face of your subject and adjust the aperture and shutter speeds until the built-in light meter needle balances,' the tutor said, smoothing his black jeans and shirt over his middle-aged paunch, his pale eyelids blinking repeatedly. 'But if you get the exposure wrong during the shooting and an Aboriginal face, say, shows too dark on the proof sheet during the printing stage, there are things you can do in the darkroom to compensate for your poor exposure.'

'What?'

'It's called dodging and burning.'

I thought momentarily of that nightmare I used to have about running from our neighbours with my father.

'If a face is too light on the print, you need to *burn* that section, by exposing it for a longer time. If a face is too dark, you need to *dodge* that section.'

'How do you do that?'

'You can use a piece of cardboard. You move it around as the print is exposed under the darkroom enlarging lamp. To burn a face that's so pale you can't see the gradations in light on it – like the woman's – let the face sit for a longer time under the enlarger's light. To dodge, use a small piece of cardboard to block light from reaching a too-dark area – say that man's face.'

In the darkroom I couldn't find any cardboard, so I used my own hand to dodge my father's face and burn my mother's. But it was imprecise and required too much trial and error. Even after I finally cut two scraps of photographic paper to the right shapes for each parent, I found burning my mother's face to the correct exposure difficult. It seemed I'd never get her right.

✳

I married one of the other students I'd met in my university photography course, and became pregnant later that year. My father seemed pleased that I'd done this in the correct order. My mother hoped for the best.

I lay awake at night listening to the low hum of the traffic on the highway that separated my mother and me, wondering how I would be able to care adequately for her after the baby arrived.

✳

Dodging and burning: photos of my mother's face after the divorce

When I finally print my mother's face correctly in the darkroom, I am shocked to see the harsh lines running from her outer nostrils to the corners of her mouth. Had they deepened because she'd wept so much recently, or was she just getting old?

I tell myself I'll have to read the light and shadows on her face more carefully when I visit her.

SONGS FROM
THE OTHER SIDE OF THE WORLD

WATCHING me breastfeed my newborn in the maternity hospital, my mother told me she never forgot the fierce gleam in my eye as I took to her breast for the first time.

'Your father said it was the Oliveira fierceness, a family determined to prevail against all odds. He was pleased you had that and were paler than him, because he thought you'd find it easier to get on in life if we migrated to Australia.' She paused thoughtfully. 'Keep that fierceness. I was never fierce enough for my own good.'

'Do you know why?'

Her brow furrowed, as it did when she was in pain. 'When I cried or called for help, my mother told me to stop being such a nuisance.'

✳

Alone in her little flat on the other side of the city, my nocturnal mother used an old milk jug in the early evenings to water the few pots of herbs, cuttings and seedlings she'd taken from the garden she'd grown with Dad. Then she'd walk in Hyde Park nearby, hoping. For what? Love, probably.

But she settled for less. Small blessings:

A broken-winged duck making headway across the lake every evening, despite the wind. On the lawn sometimes, a bottle of juice or wine left over from other people's picnics earlier in the day.

'I can't afford such luxuries,' she explained.

'You don't have to scavenge,' I said, appalled. 'I'll give you money.'

'Don't worry. It's just that I've been giving money to a few homeless people down at the park lately.'

'Mum! On your pension!'

She looked away from me, as if I didn't understand.

One evening, she found a broken eggshell in an empty nest blown down from the gnarled old trees by the first autumn squalls. As she picked it up, she felt an ache in her left breast. She mistook it for heartache. Until her fingertips found the hard lump there.

＊

After her mastectomy in the small hospital overlooking the river upstream from the city, my mother told me she felt like rubbish. At night when she thought about her future as she lay in the dark hospital ward, her heart raced arrhythmically, keeping her awake, causing the night-shift nurse to call in the doctor.

'It's probably ectopic,' he told her the next day when the test results for her heart came back negative. 'Nothing too much to worry about.'

'I thought the term ectopic was used only to describe pregnancies,' she said, glancing at me.

'Ectopic basically means external,' the doctor explained. 'It's also used to describe these kinds of heartbeat irregularities caused by things external to the heart, like emotional stress. Try not to worry. I'll see you before you're discharged.'

'It seems to me emotional stress is *central* to the heart, rather than external,' she said to me after he left.

※

My milk dries up just before I go to pick up my mother from hospital a few days later, baby in my arms.

'The stitches will dissolve. You'll need to come back and get the drain removed in a few days,' a nurse tells us. A Cancer Foundation volunteer wearing pastel clothes and a bobbed blonde hairdo gives my mother a small lambswool-filled cotton pad wrapped in pale pink tissue paper.

'A little something to slip into your bra when the scar's healed. Until you feel ready for a reconstruction.'

'Thank you so much,' my mother murmurs, before turning her face away so the volunteer can't see her tears.

'I doubt I'll ever be reconstructed,' my mother confides in me after the volunteer leaves. 'Not after so much demolition. I have no health insurance. Reconstruction costs too much.'

The baby cries and nuzzles my breast.

*

Months after she was discharged, the mastectomy wound had healed to a shiny dark pink crescent of new skin. My mother usually slept until around midday and drank several cups of tea before showering. The scar still tender to touch. She struggled with tucking the little lambswool pad securely into her bra when she dressed, only venturing out late in the afternoon or early evening to buy a few groceries or a cup of coffee.

*

'I miss having my family around me,' my mother said when I visited. 'I miss your voices.'

'Would you like to come and live with us? Or find a place closer to us?'

'No, I like having my own space. It's just the days sometimes feel a bit too empty.'

Hoping to help her overcome her losses and silences, I bought her a CD player, gave her money to buy music at the shop nearby.

'Thank you! A bit of music should help fill the emptiness,' she smiled.

※

The next time I knocked on my mother's door with her clean sheets on one hip and the baby on my other, I heard a woman singing, but couldn't make out her words even when my mother opened the door.

'What language is that?'

'Portuguese. Fado, songs of fate.'

'Are you feeling fated?'

'A bit. Apparently your father's mother used to sing fado sometimes. She must've felt pretty doomed at times, poor thing.'

'Why?'

'Your grandfather's alcoholism after the war. The aftermath of all the traumas he suffered when he was imprisoned during the Japanese Occupation.'

She'd bought other world music too. Gypsy hymns, flamenco singing, Edith Piaf. She played some flamenco songs as we changed her sheets. Whenever we changed the sheets in her new bedroom, the room was so small we had to squeeze between her old marriage bed and the wall on either side.

'They all sound like songs of loss,' I said.

'So they are,' she nodded, 'songs of loss from the other side of the world. I'll have to get out of this. Somehow.'

'Get out of what?'

'This grief.' She pulled at the top sheet so tightly there was nothing to tuck in on my side.

'Well you've lost a lot lately. The divorce. The mastectomy.'

She sat suddenly on the edge of the bed. 'I think it goes back further than that.'

'What do you mean?' I placed my hand on hers as her tears welled. She spoke only after they'd finished falling.

'I feel something else was taken from me much earlier, maybe in my infancy, before I had words to describe it. It's almost as if part of me was … *obliterated*.'

'What do you mean?'

'I have just this … memory … No. Not memory, quite. Just this sense of terror, followed by utter desolation. Those feelings have been with me as far back as I can remember.'

'You can't recall anything from your childhood that might explain them?'

'I don't think so.' She smiled wanly. 'Unless that memory's still in the darkroom developing. Apparently I lost my voice during my infancy for several months. Maybe it was related to that.'

'What caused that? An illness?'

'My parents never told me. I feel I've been trying to find my voice ever since.'

'What do you mean?'

'Trying to stand up for myself. Never mind sing.' She tugged the sheet again.

'Have you spoken to any counsellors or psychologists about it?'

'No.'

'Maybe give it a try?'

'Maybe.' Almost invisible motes of dust rose in the late afternoon sunlight coming through her curtains as we lifted the blanket by its corners and let it fall.

❊

My mother saw a few psychologists that year and next, though she could barely afford them. But even the most accomplished of them couldn't help her trace what had happened to her in infancy. She'd recount to me what they'd told her. Most of the psychologists guessed it was something to do with her parents. They would ask if she'd felt loved by them; if her mother had paid her much attention when she was little. When she'd answered no, one suggested her mother might have suffered from postnatal depression after giving birth to her younger sister, Irene.

❊

'I suspect you may have been sexually abused,' the last psychologist she sees concludes. 'But if it happened when you were pre-verbal, it's very difficult to be certain.'

My mother and I are at the café on Matilda Bay when she tells me this, overlooking the shoreline she'd walked with my father when they were courting. I nod, put my hand on hers, can't find the right words to say to her. But I'm thinking, *Please no. Not that.*

❊

My mother asked her sister if she knew anything about their upbringing that might explain her terror. Had their parents ever told her about anything traumatic that might've happened when they were little? But Aunty Irene insisted theirs had been a happy childhood.

My mother told me afterwards, 'Your grandmother always described Irene as an easy baby, trouble-free. She described me as a nuisance.'

I recoiled from her bitterness. She began speaking to me about Elvira, her orphaned grandmother. She'd felt closer to Elvira than to her own mother. She could sense that only Elvira understood her terror.

'She died just after I began school. I felt no-one would truly understand me again. In the year after she died, I kept falling over, bumping into things. As if I'd lost my bearings.'

※

In my house on the edge of Fremantle, I dreamed of having a bedroom in a house I'd never seen before, which was invaded by an intruder while I lay in bed. I had to decide whether to stay quiet so he wouldn't know I was there, or shout for help. I was so frightened that I had to gather all my courage to call out in the dream. At first I couldn't find my voice. But when I finally did, it was so loud I woke my husband, who shook me awake to quieten me.

'Sorry. Just a bad dream,' I said. 'Maybe I've inherited shouting in my sleep from Mum.'

The dream recurred a few times a year after that, replacing the dreams of falling I'd had ever since we'd left Singapore in my infancy. Houses and rooms differed from dream to dream, yet always seemed familiar. Sometimes I simply could not find my voice to call for help. Other times I managed to shout so loudly from the depths of the nightmare that I woke people sleeping nearby.

I didn't always wake straight after the nightmare and sometimes I probably forgot that I'd had it at all. It took me a few seasons to realise it was similar to the nightmares my mother had told me about years before, but the intruder in my dream never managed to reach or touch me. And my nightmare never ended with me waking to a migraine, or any other terrible pain. Only the abiding sense that I could not find the hidden cause of my mother's pain, no matter how hard I tried.

※

I'd rarely seen my father since he'd shifted earlier in the year with Trudi, from our chocolate Hydro Cream family home to their sparkling new blond-brick retirement village duplex in the far northern suburbs, miles away from my home. But one winter's evening as the rain drummed on the roof, Trudi rang to tell me his recently diagnosed Parkinson's disease had begun slurring his speech and stalling his movements so much that she'd had to put him in a nursing home.

My first visit to the nursing home. Dad confides that the only thing he likes about it is its name.

'Brightwater,' he says. 'Reminds me of … your mother. How is … she?' Why did he connect that name with her?

'Oh, she has her ups and downs,' I reply. How can I tell him the truth about her, when he might have only a few more months to live? How can I tell him her unhappiness had worsened over the years?

'She … wouldn't have … put me in a place like … this,' he murmured sadly.

Surprised, I said gently, 'Probably not.'

My father swallows the dregs of his cup of tea carefully, but some dribbles down his chin. He tries to wipe it with a serviette.

'Can't … remember exactly … why I left her.'

'No?'

'But … your mother carried on ... endlessly.'

'What d'you mean?' I take the serviette, wipe his grey-stubbled chin.

'All that … weeping,' he says. And one tear rolls slowly down his dark face, catching the light from the golden hour just drawing to a close outside.

※

My mother listened to music for hours in her flat, but not only to console herself.

She'd gradually lost her hearing completely in one ear, a condition inherited from her father that couldn't be remedied by a hearing aid. She hoped that if she listened to a lot of music, she would be able to remember melodies and songs, even if she eventually lost her hearing in the other ear too. In this way, she prepared herself for another of the deaths that would befall her before her final one. In this way and in many other unacknowledged ways, she gathered her courage.

※

I read in the daily newspaper that a psychologist at the clinic my mother attended had been accused of planting 'false memories' of childhood sexual abuse in clients' minds.

'Ah well,' my mother said when I told her as she stirred her coffee in one of her favourite cafés, overlooking the ocean north of Port Beach. 'Back to square one, I suppose.'

'What do you mean?'

'Not now please, Sally Jones. I am too tired. I wish someone wise would tell me what to do, which way to go, how to save myself.'

Then she opened her arms to her grand-daughter, now a toddler, as she climbed down from her chair and walked towards her.

※

Family likeness

I ask the waitress to photograph all three of us together on the café balcony that afternoon: my mother holding my daughter face outwards, me standing just behind them. Each of us looking out towards the sea's opalescent horizon expectantly, as if waiting for our ship to come in, or at least for the tide to turn.

THE LITTLE PALACE OF DREAMS

SHE kept opening her arms not only to her family, but to people she met on her evening walks around her new neighbourhood. The young Kenyan woman who rented the flat next to hers, the Aboriginal family at the park, the elderly Polish man downstairs who biked through Northbridge with his pet galah on his shoulder, the sad middle-aged alcoholic man smelling of cask wine who she met on the stairs some evenings. There were others I did not ever see, but whose traces I read in letters, cards and teacup dregs on her kitchen counter.

'Whole worlds,' she said, 'people contain whole worlds within them.'

*

She didn't succeed in making friends with everyone she met. A new smartly dressed Anglo-Saxon Australian neighbour with gold chains around her neck and wrists moved into the large recently renovated flat opposite hers. When Mum greeted her at the top of the stairs, the new neighbour looked her up and down disdainfully and shut her door on her.

※

My mother didn't stand for the national anthem when we found ourselves on the edge of an Anzac Day ceremony in King's Park. But she stood up for something else later that day. She saw the young Kenyan woman next door carrying boxes out of her flat. She confided that she was shifting out because the new neighbour had made life too difficult for her.

'What did she do?' Mum asked her.

'She keeps telling me to go back to where I come from.'

We saw the new well-dressed neighbour coming up the stairs a few hours later. Mum quietly told her what the Kenyan woman had said about her.

'Is this true?' Mum concluded. The new neighbour said nothing, but nodded proudly and unlocked her door.

'With all due respect. It's the twenty-first century,' my mother said to her, her voice low but wavering with anger. 'Everyone should be welcome here.'

'I paid good money to buy my apartment,' the new neighbour retorted, 'and I expect to sell it for a profit in a few years. Tenants like her will devalue my property.' Her gold jewellery and keys tinkled as she shut her door firmly.

'The most expensively dressed sometimes have the

most poverty-stricken spirits,' my mother said sadly as we descended the stairs.

※

My mother tried learning Spanish in night class for a while, but her diminished hearing made it difficult. She began buying travel guidebooks in secondhand bookshops. *Lonely Planet Spain. Berlitz Venice, Eye-Witness Paris, Insight Guide to Mexico.*

'Would you like to travel?'

'Can't afford it. But reading about the world and its people steadies my panic, somehow.'

'Where would you like to go most?'

'France or Spain I guess.'

'Why?'

'My grandmother Elvira's parents came from France and Spain, I think. But I'd settle for any place people love their neighbours, no matter where they come from.'

※

My mother began making her own world in her small flat, blutacking pictures of gilded palaces and flamenco dancers in vivid colours to the walls alongside my father's fading black and white photos of us in Singapore.

'Decorating your own little palace,' I smiled. 'Which of those places would you most like to visit?'

'Probably the Alhambra.'

'Why?'

'Because east met west there. The meeting of two civilisations, from which good things grow.'

Next to the poster of the Alhambra, she'd stuck the photo of her and Aunty Mercedes picnicking with me on the beach overlooking the South China Sea.

'You weren't like other young women you knew at university,' I said, looking at her in the photo. 'None of them married Asians, right? You were a trailblazer, even then.'

'How is your father?'

'Well. The drugs seem to be keeping his illness in check,' I said. 'For now.'

'Say hello to him from me.' She straightens the photo. 'Give him my love.'

＊

My mother began wandering from her flat for miles, trawling through neighbourhood verge clearances and opportunity shops, scrounging relics of the whims, overseas vacations and failed hobbies of the comfortable upper-middle-class homes nearby: books, pictures, designer hats, shoes, toys and anything else that might interest her grand-daughter. Lengths of discarded fabric, saris and sarongs, handicrafts and other souvenirs from Asia.

'How things have changed. Everyone seems to have been to Asia now,' she remarked.

'Balinese pool pavilions being built all around here.'

She asked me to drive her slowly around the neighbour-hood during verge clearances, stopping me to help her haul chairs, a sofa, fabric and artefacts onto the back seat and into the boot, and then up the three flights of stairs to her flat.

❋

She hung an embroidered golden sari above her bed, sarongs across the windows to keep the migraine-triggering summer glare outside. In her tiny sitting room, a round brass table she found out the back of a closed-down kebab shop, a rush-seated wooden Spanish chair, small Middle Eastern carpet and tapestry cushions. She blutacked more travel posters, reproductions of masterpieces, cuttings from magazines and pictorial calendars from years past onto the walls between the family photos and the yellowing but exuberant childhood drawings and paintings done by me years ago, and more recently by my daughter.

❋

She no longer cooked Asian or Mediterranean dishes, instead eating something with her evening cup of coffee at the local café, or snacking like a nocturnal bird on an apple or an egg or tinned sardines on a piece of toast. The toomba-toomba from Singapore stood empty on the end of her kitchen counter. But when I looked closely at the mottled interior of the toomba-toomba, I saw faint gold stains of spice and my parents' youthful enthusiasm for feeding each other delicious things.

On the small blue sofa we'd dragged in from the verge, she'd piled soft toys discarded from the neighbourhood's bygone childhoods. A tan corduroy cat with green button eyes, a sartorially dressed brown bear with one ear missing, an orange-haired ragdoll wearing a patched dress. My daughter stood breathless with excitement in the midst of all this, before scooping up the toys and throwing herself into my mother's lap. Almost buried, my mother laughed more deeply than I'd ever heard her, yet it sounded as young as my daughter's laughter. For the first time, I saw my mother's joys were as deep as her sorrows.

※

Amongst the pictures on her walls, she pasted quotes from various philosophers, commentators and mystics. Below a photo of her grand-daughter looking up at the sky, she'd pasted a quote from Simone Weil: *Love is not consolation. Love is light.*

Despite the fact that bright light often caused her pain.

※

She mostly woke late in the morning and disliked being visited until late in the afternoon. Sometimes if I dropped in late Saturday or Sunday afternoon to see if she needed anything from the shops or would like to go out for a coffee or meal, she would only open her door a crack. But I saw she was still in her dressing-gown, and I saw in her eyes that the darkness in her had risen so far she could not reach out from it.

'I think it's better if you leave,' she would say.

I knew better than to try to persuade her to come with me. But as I walked down the three flights of stairs, the panic rose in me as if I were still a child, afraid that my mother was abandoning me. Or worse, that she still wanted to die.

※

Autumn, her favourite season. After a cup of coffee at a café, my mother walked in the late afternoon chill through the fallen leaves at Hyde Park, wearing her old black coat with faux fur collar and cuffs that she'd bought at a David Jones sale just before I'd started high school. Hauling her latest opportunity shop finds in an old vinyl shopping trolley, she paused as usual to give money to the two homeless women begging alongside the path, who sometimes camped nights behind the hedge near the public toilets.

'Gimme your coat, sister,' the youngest of them beseeched her. My mother hesitated. Her oldest and favourite coat, from her married years. The only one she hadn't found abandoned on some verge.

While she took off and gave her coat to the young woman in the park, the middle-aged woman sidled behind my mother and took her purse from her handbag. My mother didn't realise this until she saw them both running away, the middle-aged woman with her purse in hand. Heart pounding, my mother called out, but they ignored her. The last of her fortnight's pension money, her B Class Widow's concession card. Worse, the photo of my daughter with her first handwritten message on the back: *Fur Grrranma with luv.*

Trembling – with cold, or was it the shock? – my mother crossed the park and walked one block home, past the wealthier neighbours oblivious, safe and warm in their comfortable homes.

Heart still beating so hard she could barely catch her breath, she walked up the stairs, fumbled in her bag for her keys. Surely they hadn't taken the keys too? There, at the bottom of her bag. Hands shaking, she opened her door, locking it behind her quickly as if keeping out the bad luck, sneakier and more agile than her.

She turned on the kettle and the CD player to calm herself, sat catching her breath and thinking about whether to phone someone for help. But her smartly dressed new neighbour in the flat opposite hers shouted, 'Turn your music down, you crazy old woman.'

My mother turned her music off and didn't call the police. She knew the thieving women in the park were probably poorer than her. She hoped for the weather and her new neighbour to turn warmer.

※

Multiple exposures

The setting sun backlighting her through her glass balcony door, haloing her silver hair. My mother the patron saint of lost things. Shivering amidst her verge clearance finds, wearing her blue woollen dressing-gown over her Indian dress because she'd just given her coat away.

Her face is too complicated to read, like a negative frame containing multiple exposures. As if she needs someone to wind the film forwards to a new, clearer future for her.

THE GARDENS OF MEMORY

MY mother gradually transforms her flat's balcony into what might be her last garden.

'The only way I can ground myself, living so high in the air,' she confides.

She draws on all the gardens of her memory to grow this little balcony garden. Its branches frame the small stone church and spire visible over the back fence of the apartment block.

'I don't go to church much anymore.'

'Why not?'

'Things have happened,' she says thoughtfully, 'that make me dislike institutionalised religion. But I still like little old churches.'

'What things have happened?'

'Never mind, Sally Jones. Don't you worry.'

※

Geranium and lavender cuttings, descended from her two earlier gardens, took root in unfamiliar territory once again and, by spring, nodded their glad pink, red, white and mauve heads. She nurtured seeds from the native shrubs she'd planted with my father around our last house; trained a cutting of its Weeping Wanderer over her balcony railings; grew basil and parsley from seed-heads she'd hastily plucked from her kitchen herb bed before she shifted. They thrived in the dappled light cast by the lemon tree in the earthenware Shanghai pot.

She hung broken strings of beads and Indian brass chimes from the balcony's peeling 1960s Flexalum canopy; coaxed a wide-spreading succulent to twine its white-flowering branches between the rusting railings. A bulb descended from the lemongrass smuggled from Singapore to flavour our curries in Australia, took root under her careful watering and erupted into a fountain of fresh beginnings, green against the glare of that summer and all the forgetting she was unable to do.

※

Sometimes she asked me to take her to Port Beach, but never to swim.

'That's where your father and I embarked for Singapore, alone each time,' she said, pointing to the port. 'And here's where we walked once during our courtship. And here's where you built sandcastles, and where he sometimes took you to swim,' she said as we collected shells and seaweed for her garden. And she drew a circle around my daughter building sandcastles and daydreaming in her own little world.

※

I hardly noticed over the next few years, that on the far end of her balcony, totally unsheltered from the sun, my mother grew cacti and other drought-resistant plants. But after three summers, they flowered spectacularly against the hot brick wall, huge white, yellow and pink blooms.

'They smell like the Singaporean wet markets did during the hottest months,' she said.

Around the base of many of her plants, she arranged the fragments of terracotta pots from our old family home, cracked or broken under the pressure of shifting house, marriage disintegration and other accidents. These fragments suggested a history of ruin that initially shocked or puzzled the few occasional visitors to her flat, but sometimes enchanted them. As they enchanted me when I finally brought myself to look carefully at how determined she'd been to create something new from loss and breakage.

But the smartly dressed neighbour in the flat opposite my mother's, now the secretary of Council of Owners of that block of flats, took offence at my mother's flourishing balcony garden. At their annual general meeting, she successfully moved to have my mother completely remove her balcony and its garden, claiming it was unsightly and did not meet Australian safety standards.

I took photos of the balcony and garden and sent it to the lawyer who'd befriended her during her divorce.

'Well, I wouldn't tap-dance on that balcony,' he responded to my emailed photographs. 'But it doesn't look beyond repair.'

The lawyer wrote a letter appealing the Council of Owners' request, but my mother had to use her meagre pension savings and money I gave her to pay a handyman thousands of dollars to bring the balcony 'up to standard'.

※

During the balcony repairs, the temporary shift into her living room of her pot plants tinged the light coming in through her windows green. She had no balcony garden to wander out to in her nightgown during her solitary hours. The light shifted almost imperceptibly across those weeks towards winter.

'It won't be the same. All the birds have flown away,' she mourned in the cold light.

※

Over the weeks after the balcony was repaired, she pain-stakingly rearranged her pot plants and memories of her gardens past. And the birds did come back, and her final garden sent out new shoots and flourished again under her arthritic, wrinkled but still tender hands, as if spring had come early and meant to stay.

Images almost forgotten

My mother doesn't tap-dance in her reconstructed balcony garden. But she does a slow-slippered shuffle and curtseys to the nodding heads of her geraniums and the new green shoots of rosemary screening the little church spire beyond.

'Without water and light, a garden does not grow,' she tells my daughter as they water the plants on the balcony together, using the dented milk jug filled at the kitchen tap.

'More baths for the birds!' my seven-year-old daughter shouts.

So between the plants, my mother nestles and fills her chipped and cracked old family china dishes with water. More bodies of water, vessels damaged but not broken. They will reflect the sky and the small fleeting birds that fly in and out of her days, changing seasons and all those gardens of her memories.

MY MOTHER'S LOST MEMORY

AN echo long-suppressed insisted on surfacing in my mother around that time, something more significant and deeper yet more hidden than all her other memories. And darker, much darker.

She told me that she now felt sure her increasingly frequent recurrent nightmare came from something that had happened when she was too young to speak, and that therefore maybe only her parents might know for sure what it was.

My mother hadn't seen her parents for years, after her last psychologist had suggested she should have a break from them. It seemed clear to her she must ask them questions about her infancy.

'Before it's too late,' she told me.

But incidents in the present kept interrupting her attempts to shine a light on that dark past.

My Aunty Irene rang me to say their father had been rushed to hospital. He had fallen and injured his head against the glass shelves of Myer's crockery department when looking for some Royal Doulton teacups to give my grandmother for an anniversary present. My aunty didn't tell me if any china had been broken, but it seemed he'd lost his short-term memory with the blood that flowed from his wound.

I rang my mother.

'Yes, of course I will visit him. Yes, now, I will be ready.'

※

My grandfather lay still and pale in his hospital bed, his blue eyes closed, the red of his blood-soaked bandage the only brightness. We watched the shadows elongate outside his small window. When my mother put her hand on his as she rose to leave, he opened his eyes. They looked cloudy, but he sounded surprisingly lucid.

'Ah, how are you darling? I worry you bury your light under a bushel, but I suppose it's no wonder,' he told her, before closing his eyes again and easing into sleep as the ward lights dimmed.

'Maybe it's as simple as that,' she said to me in the car as I drove her home. 'Maybe that's been my problem all these years.'

※

Over the next day, my grandfather's lungs filled with something other than air.

'Pneumonia, the old man's helper,' the nurse told us when we visited the next evening. We heard the tugboats ushering in the cargo ships at the port; sat beside him hoping for the best, but he did not open his eyes. We listened to his breathing. 'And something else,' the nurse said as she checked his pulse. 'Listen. You can hear the death rattle in his breathing.'

We listened to it through the night. It stopped just as we heard the first tugboat of the new morning usher a ship from the port out towards the open sea.

※

Within weeks of my grandfather's death, my grandmother's heart faltered badly.

'A pacemaker is your only option,' the cardiologist told her.

But the day after my grandmother's operation, Aunty Irene rang me to let me know my grandmother's frail soft body had rejected the hard plastic and metal pacemaker the cardiac team inserted. Nothing could be done medically for her heart.

※

They transfer my grandmother to a nursing home, to wait for the day her heart will stop beating altogether.

When I give Mum the news, she asks immediately to visit her.

We sidle quietly into her nursing home room to see my

grandmother, pale as a porcelain doll propped against the pillows, her eyes closed, a filigree of fine blue veins on her eyelids. My mother puts her hand gently on hers. Opening her eyes, my grandmother's face brightens with relief when she sees her. I stand near the door as Mum sits in the chair and holds her hand.

'I am so sorry!' my grandmother sobs to Mum. 'For the way I ... treated you when you were ... only a toddler.'

'No need to apologise,' Mum tells her gently. Then, even more quietly: 'What happened when I was a toddler?' The semi-transparent nylon curtain lifts and drops in the breeze.

'It wasn't that I ... did anything to you. It was what I ... didn't do. Because I was too ... guilty and ... upset. Forgive me. I was too ... traumatised to care for you in the way I should've ever since that ... terrible ... incident, and now ...' My grandmother puts her hand over her heart, grimaces. 'I am too weak to tell you ... what it was.' She closes her eyes as tears leak from their corners. She falls asleep a few minutes later. Mum holds her hand as the curtain settles, the shadows lengthen into darkness and visiting hours finish.

❋

My aunty rang the next morning to say my grandmother had died at four, just before dawn. It seemed we'd never know what had happened to Mum that had pained my grandmother so much the last time she spoke to her.

But a few months after my grandmother's funeral, on an

ordinary autumn afternoon in an ordinary café on the edge of the port city, Mum's sister revealed to her the terrible incident my grandmother hadn't been able to tell my mother about before she died.

※

Elspeth is two and a half years old, Irene four months. They'd been living a few months in a weatherboard house on the edge of a small wheatbelt town where their father Harry Green works as the town clerk.

Mrs Marjorie Green returns from the shops pushing her two infant daughters in a pram, after buying groceries for the evening meal. It's a humid summer afternoon, unbearably sticky. The sky glares down on the small trio, but darkens and rumbles with thunder to the north, above the ripening wheatfields. The fields ripple and shiver in gusts of wind as the storm approaches fast. She hurries to the outskirts of town, where the distance between the houses lengthens and the bush begins. She reaches their small house between the town's backblocks and the bush; thunder rumbles again and the baby cries to be fed. Pain in her breasts as the milk comes in, the first drops of rain on her neatly bobbed hair, Marjorie drags the pram onto the front verandah, puts the toddler Elspeth in the sleep-out cot for her afternoon nap and takes the pram and baby Irene inside.

She fills the kettle and heats it, hears Elspeth whimpering from her cot on the verandah sleepout. This isn't unusual.

Her firstborn often does this when she is put in the cot for her afternoon nap. Glad the storm seems to be receding, Marjorie disregards Elspeth's crying, puts the meat and milk in the fridge, makes herself a cup of tea when the kettle boils and sits feeding the baby.

Her firstborn's crying rises suddenly to a crescendo on the verandah. Her second daughter still feeding hungrily at her breast, Marjorie calls out loudly to Elspeth to hush. But the toddler's screaming doesn't stop. Finally, baby Irene dozes off to sleep on the breast. Marjorie puts her in the cot in the master bedroom. She hears footsteps running away from the house and hurries to the verandah to hush the toddler and to call out to the visitor she'd just missed.

But the visitor has disappeared, and fast. A dazzlingly bright ray of sunlight appears from behind a receding storm cloud, shining in her firstborn's face. For a few seconds Marjorie thinks maybe Elspeth's crying because the glare's hurting her eyes. Yes, that must be it. But then the young mother glimpses something else on her child. She is dumbstruck by what she sees. Her firstborn's red mouth is wide open as she screams, but much redder and wider is the glistening liquid spreading through her nappy, which is unaccountably open beneath her. The mother sees it is blood, and that it's coming from between her toddler's thighs. At first she can't understand why, stumbles closer towards the incomprehensible bleeding, wonders fleetingly if the nappy pins somehow have opened and caused the injury. Then she sees the two unbloodied safety pins are open on the verandah boards, about an adult's arm length from the cot. She sees the blood spilling from between Elspeth's short thighs and spreading from the nappy to the bright white sheets.

※

They couldn't remember who found Marjorie Green and her toddler sobbing and huddled together on the verandah, who ran to fetch Harry Green from the town clerk's office in the middle of the small wheatbelt town. He bundled his little family into the car and drove to the regional hospital over an hour away. No-one knew in those days how to treat such a wound in an infant, apart from washing it and applying iodine, and no-one knew what to do for her pain or her mother's.

The police kept the bloodied nappy and sheets as evidence for a crime they would never solve. The young family transferred out as soon as Elspeth recovered enough to travel, back to the wheatbelt town where my grandparents had courted, so Elspeth's grandmother Elvira could help care for her; change her nappies and bathe her little body frequently and tenderly to prevent infection, feed her broth and delicacies to help the injury heal.

Elspeth's parents followed the advice of that town's doctor, who said their firstborn was so young she would have no memory of her *violation*. Relying on his advice, they decided it would be best never to tell Elspeth. And so they kept their grim silence until my grandmother, only days away from her death over six decades later, told my mother's sister Irene the story.

✻

Finally I could begin to understand why my grandparents had reacted with such consternation to my mother's problems as an adult: her depressions and her unhappy marriage might've suggested to them that they had failed to erase all consequences of that hidden chapter of her infancy, that it had stained their daughter's life as indelibly as it had stained the sheets on which she'd been violated.

✻

Bodies of water carry memories, long after violent storms and their waves have subsided, long after the ripples become invisible.

'That white-hot pain followed by darkness whenever I faint or have migraines. Some part of me must've remembered being raped as an infant. But why tell me now, when I am an old woman?' my mother wept after she told me about the hidden chapter her sister had finally revealed to her.

I had no adequate reply. I had no remedy for her anguish. And despite my shock, I felt sorry for my aunty, too. She would've felt she'd be damned if she told my mother, and damned if she didn't, I guess.

✻

The night my mother tells me about her sister's revelation, I have the recurring nightmare again: an intruder enters my home while I am in bed. This home has changed again from the last time I'd had the dream, but in it, I am alone when the intruder comes. This time, the longest part of the nightmare involves struggling to overcome my fear enough to shout for help. This time when I finally find my voice, I shout more loudly than I ever have before and wake myself. I lie there, realising I've been screaming for help on my mother's behalf.

I think about her as I try to sleep again. I think about how people sometimes judge her harshly, misinterpret her depression, confusion and anxiety. *Crazy old woman.*

All her life she's been bewildered by this abiding sense of unhealed rupture, and now its cause has become clear, she has to find a way of coping with that.

Who will shine a light on how I can help my mother now?

※

Unexposed frames

Near the end of any spool of film used in old single lens reflex cameras, some frames always remain unexposed, impossible to read as anything but darkness after the film's been developed.

MENTAL HEALTH
FOR OLDER ADULTS

IN the years immediately following the revelation of her rape as an infant, my aging mother sometimes feared the weight of it might drive her mad. We both spoke to psychologists about it. I rang a sexual assault referral centre and another psychologist, but they all told us how difficult it was to address rape that had occurred to a pre-verbal infant. My mother's migraines, nightmares and depression grew more intense and frequent.

'Shall we try to find a good doctor?'

'I've already tried a few. All they do is give me medication for the migraines and antidepressants for the depression. But the migraines and depression keep coming.'

※

My mother tried to calm herself by making something new from abandoned things. Her parents had left their Queen

Anne china cabinet to her, but she did not put china in it. She placed family photographs on the top shelf, statues of Indian gods and goddesses and Chinese calligraphy on the middle shelf with our childhood drawings. She fashioned hearts from wire found on the verge and filled them with petals from her garden; wove nests from twigs found in the park. These she put on the cabinet's lower shelves. The cabinet seemed to me a kind of diorama of her life. The nests appeared empty, but they carried dreams of her past and future.

※

Struggling with a demanding new teaching job, I did not know that my mother's depression came to a head on the same day as a strange abscess on her upper back. Both of them in a place beyond her reach, and in the middle of my busiest ever working weeks.

A new GP at her local surgery tried to squeeze the mess out of her, lancing the abscess efficiently enough. But when she'd squeezed some of Mum's story about her infant rape out of her, the GP looked as if wished she could push it all back in again. The GP took off her rubber gloves, washed her hands punctiliously after cleaning up the abscess, but had nothing except a small box of pills to treat my mother's sadness.

'Let's see if this antidepressant works better for you. Take one right now,' she instructed her. The little white pill with the line down the middle; its name like an imperative or a sword.

Effexor. 'I'll write a referral to mental health professionals who can help you with some of your issues.'

※

After she told me that on the phone, I kept my fingers crossed, marked and prepared lessons all weekend and planned to see Mum the following weekend, finally ringing her again late on Sunday before my teaching week. She sounded brighter than she had for months.

'Three days on those antidepressants and I feel happier, I have to admit.'

'That's brilliant, Mum. I'll ring you tomorrow after work to see how you're getting on.'

I rang all the next evening but she didn't answer. Maybe she was out late walking as usual after her evening coffee at the nearby café. Maybe she was chatting with the waitresses she'd befriended over the years. Maybe she didn't hear the phone ringing. Exhausted, I went to bed soon after my daughter, knowing nothing about the visitors to my mother's flat earlier that sunny spring Monday.

※

Her new GP had mentioned to my mother only a referral to 'mental health professionals', not a surprise visit from them.

At 9.30, my mother thought she heard someone knocking at her door. She twisted her silver hair hastily into a bun, shoved her hearing aid in. Yes, it was definitely someone at her door. How long had they been knocking?

When she opened the door slightly, taking care to keep her nightie hidden, her strange visitors looked cross. As if they'd already decided to make her pay for keeping them waiting. One in a nurse's uniform, one in a navy blue skirt suit; the heavy foundation on their faces fissuring slightly with disapproval. The suited one looked at her watch and stepped over the threshold. Without invitation, right up close.

'Elspeth Elvira Olivera?' she enunciated loudly with her pale lipsticked mouth.

'That's me,' my mother replied.

'I'm Dr Blake. We work in the Mental Health Unit for Older Adults team.' Dr Bleak, my mother thought, as the visitors' beady eyes scrutinised her. 'Your GP's worried about you. She sent us a referral.'

Following Dr Bleak's eyes down her nightie, my mother drew her arms across her chest, wishing she could disappear altogether. Her nightdress was stained, its collar deliberately slashed so it wouldn't give her neck pain. The nurse's nostrils twitched as she sidled past my mother to the kitchen, opening the fridge and cupboard doors.

'Are you looking for something?' my mother asked.

Neither of them replied. The nurse headed for the bathroom. Was she rummaging through the vanity cabinet? My mother wished she'd concealed her Poise Pads and stained lambswool brassiere insert.

When the nurse returned from the bathroom, my mother stepped back. She hadn't had her morning shower yet, and was wearing the same nightie she'd worn for two nights, stained by the Seasol she'd poured on her pot plants that morning.

'How about coming with us? For a little rest. We have a nice room for you,' the doctor said. She and the nurse each grasped one of my mother's elbows, hemming her in, manoeuvring her towards the door.

'I don't need a nice little room. I'm quite happy here, thank you.'

But Dr Bleak said, 'Your GP doesn't think so.'

'She's new to me. Doesn't know me well.' But they disregarded this.

'Your nightdress looks … filthy,' said the nurse. 'We'll give you a nice clean one.'

'Liquid fertiliser,' my mother explained. 'Seasol.'

There in her little flat with its fading pictures of the world's peoples and her own family, my mother felt the firm grip of the mental health team through her threadbare nightie sleeve. She wondered if maybe they really could help her get past her sadness.

'As long as it's only a little while. But please give me a chance to shower and get changed.'

'You don't need to,' the doctor insisted.

'And pack my bag with a change of clothes and a few bits and pieces.'

'You don't need anything,' said the nurse. 'Just your keys, Social Security and Medicare cards.'

'They're in my handbag.' She reached out to her handbag on the table.

'Just bring that.' Their grip on her tightened as they steered her through the door and slammed it shut after her.

'But my clothes. My toothbrush. The things I need every day.'

'You don't need anything,' the doctor repeated.

They walk her down three flights of stairs towards a sparkling white Holden with Western Australian government number plates. The embarrassment of walking past the smartly dressed neighbour and onto the street in her stained nightdress and slippers.

The car's back seat smelled of Pine O Cleen and something else, as if someone's vomit had been recently cleaned from it. The nurse clicked the safety belt shut over my mother's nightie and sat next to her in the back seat.

'My garden needs watering.' The herbs under the potted lemon tree still bearing the last of its winter fruit, the shy bulbs emerging from the terracotta flowerpots to the sunlight.

'Don't worry about your garden. We'll take care of everything.' How smoothly Doctor Bleak shifted through the gear changes, despite heavy traffic.

'Where are we going?'

'A nice little place not far away.'

'Why?'

'Don't worry. We'll take care of everything.'

The car pulled up outside a smug faux-Federation-style building directly next to the hospital where she'd had her mastectomy years before. Blond brick, heritage green fretwork above the porch. A brass panel announcing the name of the Health Minister who'd *opened this facility in 1999*. The nurse tapped numbers on a metal box next to the door. The automatic frosted glass doors hissed open onto a grey foyer. Inside, my mother turned to look behind her, glimpsed a lone dove descending from the bright blue sky as the frosted glass doors hissed closed behind them. Ahead, a glass-fronted office with no person or lights on, and a laminated pamphlet stand. One of the pamphlets read:

VOLUNTARY PATIENTS. YOUR RIGHTS UNDER THE

MENTAL HEALTH ACT

Was she voluntary or involuntary? She reached out for the pamphlet, but the nurse steered her away from it. More green and pink jigsaw-patterned brochures:

COMMUNITY TREATMENT ORDERS. CARERS.

ELECTRO-CONVULSIVE THERAPY.

Would someone help her make sense of the jigsaw? Doctor Bleak only gripped my mother's other arm more firmly and punched more numbered metal buttons on a beige door which opened with a double click, like a bank safe.

Did my mother feel involuntary? Did she wonder if she had any voice or power in this new nightmare?

On the other side of the door, Dr Bleak steered her into

the surprisingly small hands of an amply girthed middle-aged nurse, before retreating swiftly back through the door. WINNIE. NURSE COORDINATOR, her badge read. Winnie took my mother's handbag and emptied it over the desk; put her wallet, watch, keys, Quick-Eze and address book into a large transparent Glad Bag and locked it in a safe.

'We'll keep this at reception,' said Winnie, eyeing the handbag's grimy handles with distaste. 'Follow me.' She has small feet to go with her hands, but her muscular calves bulged like bottles from her little white shoes which squeaked all the way to the end of the corridor. They entered a room smelling of antiseptic. A sunflower wilted in a tall blue plastic vase on a small table next to a white-sheeted bed.

Winnie bundled my mother into the adjoining bathroom. It was whiter than any bathroom she'd been in before. All the towels were labelled WA HEALTH DEPARTMENT. Winnie pulled her nightie off her, wrinkling her nose and sniffing.

'Are you incontinent?'

'No. The stains are just fertiliser. Seasol.'

'Well. Make sure you wash yourself properly. Put on this hospital gown after. And the paper panties.' Winnie slammed the door and left my mother staring at the reflection of her old body in a huge mirror, her mastectomy scar pink in the fluorescent light. She'd never seen herself naked under such harsh light. She showered, shivering despite the warm water.

When she stepped out of the bathroom with the thin blue polyester hospital gown crooked across her gaunt shoulders,

Winnie was waiting next to the bedside chair, brandishing a pair of scissors and a plastic sheet.

'Sit here.' She undid my mother's bun and in a few swift swipes, cut her long hair. Years of pale silver rain fell around my mother's shoulders. 'There. That's much better.' Winnie grunted as she bundled up the hair in the plastic sheet from the floor, before leaving my mother alone in the room again.

A man, my mother thought with shock when she saw herself in the mirror, the nurse has made me look like a man.

Wearing only the paper panties like a disposable nappy, the hospital gown thin as a cheap polyester shower curtain, my mother walked down the corridor unsure of where to go, passing other old people wandering aimlessly past the locked exit door. A paunchy old man, his face peppered with liver spots, kept rearranging two chairs nearby. He gripped her by the wrist surprisingly strongly as she passed.

'Sit!' he ordered.

'Just ignore Bill,' an old woman with mauve-rinsed hair shouted to my mother through her toothless gums, 'he's got OCD. Always trying to organise everyone and everything.'

'C'mon Bill, *Days of Our Lives* is on TV,' said a male nurse, freeing my mother's wrist.

'Do you know where I can get some proper clothes?' my mother asked.

'Cupboard's over there behind the nurse,' replied the toothless woman.

'Just take one set of clothes,' said Nurse Coordinator,

opening the cupboard door. Pilled flannelette shirts, over-washed polyester blend windcheaters and vests, tracksuit pants with the drawstrings removed.

'Which ones are the ladies'?' my mother asked.

'They're all unisex.' Winnie impatiently handed her a navy-striped windcheater and a mustard coloured pair of tracksuit pants. 'One size fits all,' she said, hurrying into the TV room.

'They seem a bit big,' my mother said, looking at the waistband of the pants.

'They take out the strings so no-one'll hang themselves. That's why we don't have phones in our rooms. Or so they say, but it's probably just another cost-cutting measure. Name's Betty. Betty Blue.' The woman pointed to her dyed hair.

My mother took the second-hand polyester clothes to her room, pulled them on. No bra and no lambswool pad to wear against her mastectomy scar. And so thirsty. Hot and cold water taps in the bathroom, but no drinking glass.

'Can I have a glass of water?' she asked the male nurse in the corridor.

'Sorry, no sharp things allowed in your room. Get you a plastic cup after lunch. Follow me.'

He sat my mother in the dining room, between Betty and a tiny pale whispering woman my mother couldn't hear.

'Her name's June,' shouted Betty. Both women chewed Vegemite and cheese white bread sandwiches and shoved Family Assorted biscuits into their mouths as if they were in a race, washing them down with a plastic cup each of powdered Caterer's Blend tea. 'Take more biscuits,' Betty shouted at my mother, smuggling a few into her pocket.

'I don't like this kind of biscuit much,' my mother replied.

'The meals are so bad and small here you gotta learn to eat more bickies.' Betty lowered her voice. 'Do you know the code?' she murmured to my mother.

'Pardon?'

'The code to get out.' Betty beckoned and took her over to the beige door, pointed to the little numbered metal buttons on the panel next to it.

'No. Sorry.'

'What are you in for?'

'Not sure. I was found wanting in some way, I suppose.'

'When d'yer get out?'

'I don't know. Just got in. How about you?'

'How can I know that when I haven't even figured out why I'm here? Two weeks and they still won't tell me. This is some kind of prison, and we're its prisoners. Get so fucking tired sitting around doing nothing all day, yer just want to go to bed early.'

※

A fresh-faced, slightly balding man in a suit visited my mother in her room that afternoon, after armchair exercises and bingo.

'I'm Tim Smith,' he said, extending his hand and shaking hers. 'I'm your psychiatrist while you're here.'

'An ordinary name,' she observed. 'But not such an ordinary man, I suspect.'

Tim Smith blushed.

'Are you the chief psychiatrist?'

'No,' Tim Smith smiled. 'He's way too busy to come in here. Any more questions?'

'Any more *questions*? I don't know how to begin.' She looked down at her pale calves protruding from the too short tracksuit pants. 'Why did they bring me here?'

'You'll be assessed.'

'For what?'

He opened a cardboard folder. 'Your GP diagnosed depression. Do you ever harbour suicidal thoughts?'

'No.'

'Do you ever hear voices in your head?'

'No.'

'So tell me a bit about yourself,' he said, quite kindly. 'Why are you depressed?'

'Because I'm here.'

'But you were depressed before now. Your GP mentioned you'd been abused as a child.'

'I found out only recently that I was raped when I was a toddler. But you can't do anything about that, can you?' She pushed away the memory of her dying mother's unfinished apology.

'Psychological counselling can help.'

'I've seen more psychologists and counsellors than I can count over the years.'

'Did they help?'

'Well. They knew how to open the wound up, but they weren't so good at helping it heal.'

'You'll be seeing our psychologist Clare White while you're in here. How's the Effexor going?'

'It seemed to lift my spirits slightly for the first three days.'

'And then?'

'Well, then they brought me here. And I must say since being here, I've felt more depressed than I have for years.'

'We'll increase your dose. Usually takes a bit of adjustment.'

※

'Service, service!' Bill shouted, prowling the corridor outside her room that first evening.

'Service? You have to pay for that 'ere,' quipped a white-haired Aboriginal man through his open doorway.

'The only place you can walk around here is in the corridors, with all the other drugged old zombies and loonies,' Betty said. 'At least it keeps your circulation going.'

My mother wanted to ask Betty if she meant blood or social circulation, but let Betty lead her by the hand to the television-room. The Aboriginal man played darts against the wall opposite the television. The other inmates sank like fallen monuments in front of Channel 7's sensationalised news of the outside world; except for a much younger man sitting in the corner with his grey windcheater hood pulled down over his face.

'He's in the wrong place,' Betty murmured. 'Aren't we all.'

My mother had never liked the news on commercial television stations. She kept pacing the corridor until dinner time. She sat between Betty and June in the dining room again, each chewing on a thick wodge of stale pastry around a shrivelled morsel of mince, a teaspoon of peas and a slice of white bread. Her plastic knife snapped when she tried to cut through the pastry, so she moved straight to dessert, a small child-sized tub of Peter's ice-cream. *The health food of a nation.* My mother didn't particularly like Peter's ice-cream, but it was the best part of the meal.

My mother put on the scratchy blue polyester gown and went to bed early, missing her soft cotton nightdress. Her reflux was worse than it had ever been; she wished she'd thought to get her Quick-Eze out of her handbag before they'd locked it away.

※

A night-shift nurse peered through her door's glass spy-panel every hour; the woman patient across the corridor cried *Mummy, Mummy* all night. My mother couldn't help but weep for the tenderness the woman might once have received from her mother. She lay awake until a solitary black crow called outside her window before dawn.

She finally dozed and dreamed of the Singaporean and Western Australian gardens of her past growing into one another and propagating new species of fruit she could not reach, until a loud knock on the door woke her again.

'Shower and out for breakfast,' called a trim new nurse officiously from under a permed helmet of hair.

My mother deliberately wet the mustard tracksuit pants with the shower water.

'Why are you taking so long?' the nurse said through the observation panel when she saw my mother sitting on the edge of the bed.

'I wet my trousers.'

'What, pissed on them?'

'Showered them. Can I have some fresh clothes, please?'

The nurse reappeared a few minutes later with a grey pair of tracksuit pants. My mother read her badge. KIMMY!

'Quicksticks,' Kimmy snapped, throwing her a pair of Confidence padded paper pants. 'Breakfast'll be over soon and the occupational therapist'll be doing armchair exercises and bingo in the lounge. Then you'll see the psychologist.'

My mother felt the lightning flashes of a migraine coming on. "Can you please tell me. Has someone told my daughter I am here? And how long will I be here?'

'How long's a piece of string?' Kimmy muttered, slamming the door on her way out.

✳

'So you've been depressed nearly all your adult life,' Clare White nodded at their first session, her face innocent and fresh as a baby's. 'Do you think the latest bout of depression was triggered by finding out about your ... abuse as a child?'

My mother couldn't bring herself to tell it all again.

'Don't know,' she lied. 'Just life's ups and downs, I guess.'

※

In the Mental Health Unit for Older Adults, her dreams seemed more real than her waking hours. In the darkest hour just before her second dawn in the ward, she had a dream about my father. She'd just had open-heart surgery, but he left her on a harbour bridge in a strange city, said he had to catch his ship. She looked in vain for a paper streamer to throw him as his ship approached the bridge. Anything to prolong the connection.

The stitches burst over her heart. A long red streamer erupted from it just after the ship passed beneath the bridge. But he didn't see it and didn't look up. Missed the boat again, she thought as his ship sailed from the harbour to the stormy ocean.

My mother woke, thinking she had to get better quickly so he would love her again, felt a new sense of purpose at this. Until she saw the label WA HEALTH DEPARTMENT on the hem of her bed sheets, remembered where she was. Kimmy the nurse waved at her and tapped her wristwatch on the other side of the glass spy-panel in the door.

＊

After a breakfast of pale toast and powdered instant tea, she asked Kimmy if she could ring me.

'You can use the patients' mobile phone. If it's not flat,' snapped Kimmy, handing her the little black rectangle. 'It's shared between all patients, so keep your calls short.'

'I've never used a mobile phone before.'

'Just press this red button and then the numbers.'

My mother took the phone into her room, but realised she'd forgotten my phone number. It was on the green piece of paper next to her phone at home. She'd have to find a way to get out of this place all by herself.

＊

Facelessness

In the ensuite mirror, it seems her features have vanished. Only the white glare of the mental health unit, her migraine, and utter, unremitting over-exposure. Unfaceable.

THE CODE

BEFORE I went to dial my mother's home phone yet again the next evening after work, I heard the recorded drawl of a man on my answer machine, so broad I could barely make out his words. He didn't leave a phone number. *Mental Health Unit for Older Adults.* Is that what he said? I flicked through the phone directory for these words, rang all six of the numbers listed under that heading. A male nurse answered the sixth number. Yes, they had my mother there.

I drove as fast as I could through the peak-hour traffic alongside the river. As I parked, I wondered how she'd felt to find herself back in the grounds of the old hospital where she'd had her mastectomy. I pushed the electronic bell on the front door of the newer faux-Federation building, spoke into the intercom.

Some faceless person buzzed me through the door. A nurse showed me to my mother's room. Her plastic name tag read WINNIE. NURSE COORDINATOR.

My mother sat on the edge of her bed watching the lights come on in the houses of the wealthy across the river. Her shorn hair revealed her thin neck, pale apart from a scattering of freckles at her nape from her years in the wheatbelt and in Singapore.

'My beautiful mother.'

She turned slowly to face me, like someone dreaming or heavily drugged. 'Sally Jones,' my mother said, her face almost white, her voice and hands trembling. 'You've come to rescue me again.'

Complicated depression and over-dependency, I read on my mother's observation file, maybe accidentally left by staff on the chair. Over-dependency? After living alone for so long?

'I want to take my mother home,' I told the nurse.

'Not so fast. She's still being assessed. The occupational therapist has to assess her for competency,' Winnie said officiously.

'Competency?'

'In self-care.'

'I've been looking after myself for years,' my mother said.

'Kitchen competency.'

'So long as you don't want a gourmet meal,' my mother said, only the hint of her old smile in the corners of her mouth.

'And hygiene. Bathroom competency.'

'Bathroom competency?'

'Observe you showering. To make sure you can clean yourself thoroughly.'

My mother's hand went involuntarily to her mastectomied chest. Please God, don't let them watch her naked.

'When will they assess her for competency?'

'That's up to them.'

※

At work the next day, I go through the motions of teaching my students. My mother has been invaded again, all her privacy lost, I think as I wait for one class to file out of the classroom and the next to enter. I've got to get my mother out of that place as soon as I can. Please. Please. Please.

I feel as if I am praying, but I have no-one to pray to.

※

I drove to the mental health facility as soon as I'd finished teaching for the day.

'She's still being assessed,' a new nurse told me.

How to make a cup of tea in front of a stranger. How to boil an egg in front of a stranger. How to shower naked in front of a stranger, despite her age and mastectomy. She did it all.

※

The following day, they called me in to *discuss your mother's case* before discharging her. I sat in a white boardroom at a huge table next to my little mother, facing two doctors, a psychiatrist, a social worker, a counsellor and the nurse called Kimmy.

'Why was my mother brought here in the first place?' I asked Tim Smith, the psychiatrist.

'Her referring GP said she was depressed.'

'She sounded happy when I spoke to her on her home phone after she'd taken the antidepressants for a few days.'

The psychiatrist looked embarrassed. 'A bit of overreaction on the part of the admitting doctor. Apparently her home looked a bit strange inside.'

'Unusual but clean,' I said. 'She's creative. She decorates on a budget, you could say.'

'But her assessments show she's perfectly competent.' Tim Smith beamed at her. 'Not found wanting in any way. You have to make sure you don't present as less competent than you really are,' he said, patting her on the back of her hand. 'Well. Any more questions?'

'No.'

'I have a meeting with the Chief Psychiatrist about some other matters now. Best wishes to you both.' He bowed slightly and hurried off.

Kimmy handed back my mother's watch, wallet, address book and handbag, and a new blister pack of assorted pills. Effexor, Panadeine, Osteo Ease.

'One week's supply.' Since coming here, my mother had probably swallowed more pills per day than she'd had in her life. 'You'll need to get this prescription filled at your chemist before the Webster pack runs out.'

'Can I have my nightdress back?' my mother asked.

'We sent it to the incinerator,' said Kimmy peremptorily. 'It was filthy and threadbare.'

'How can I give you back these clothes if I have nothing of my own to wear home?'

'Just return them when you see someone from our team next.'

'But I won't be seeing anyone from here again, will I?' She couldn't keep the panic from her voice.

'Another social worker and a psychologist will take over as your caseworkers. Visit you once a fortnight at your home.'

'Caseworkers? How long will I be a case? How long will they keep visiting?'

'For as long as they think you need it,' said Kimmy.

'I do not wish anyone to visit me at home.'

'You're in the system now. Follow-up appointments are compulsory. The only other option is for you to visit here in the outpatients building next door.'

'I'd prefer that.'

'You must come once a fortnight at your appointment times, or else we'll have to send someone to your home again. Come along now.'

Betty Blue stood at the end of the corridor, waving forlornly at us.

'They won't let me out because I'm forgetting too much,' Betty confided in us. My mother put her hand on Betty's but the nurse punched in the door-code, opened it and steered Mum out by her elbow to the foyer. My mother reached out for the pamphlet titled VOLUNTARY PATIENTS. YOUR RIGHTS UNDER THE MENTAL HEALTH ACT, but the nurse led her firmly away.

'Don't forget to come to your appointments.' The nurse pushed another button, released us through the hissing frosted glass doors.

My mother breathed deeply her first unconditioned air for days. Spring had almost turned to summer while she'd been on the ward. The sun burned in the birdless blue sky. In the car, she turned back just once to look at the pseudo-Federation homestead facade of the prison she'd just escaped.

'I hope all my new friends will get out soon,' she said as I accelerated to put it all behind us.

※

The ill-fitting tracksuit pants hung from her like a sleeping bag as I led her up the stairs to her flat. On her kitchen counter, mould grew in the cup of tea she'd not had time to drink before the doctor and the nurse took her away. I boiled the kettle to make her first pot of real tea in many days. But of course, the milk in the fridge was off. We took a cup of black tea each out to her little balcony. Most of the herbs had died. Even the Eureka lemon tree was wilting in its Shanghai pot.

'How are you feeling, Mum?'

'Well. Not exactly free.'

'Can you tell me why?'

'Any minute, any day, they might come knocking on my door to assess me again.'

'That psychiatrist promised me they won't.'

'I've learned not to trust their promises.'

'At least you're home.'

She didn't smile. 'But I no longer feel safe here. I won't feel free to wear my old nightdresses as late into the day as I like. Or speak honestly to any doctor, for fear of being taken away again.'

'Let's water the garden.'

'What remains of it.'

'Enough to begin a new one with.'

⁕

My mother remained anxious and jittery for weeks after her stay in the mental health unit.

'What would help you feel calmer?' I asked her.

'Maybe music and gardening? And more Quick-Eze,' she said, 'for the reflux.'

'You could come and live with us.'

'I need my own space. I'm used to it now.'

I gave her money to buy more music CDs and took her to

nurseries to buy plants to replace the dead ones. She bought Heart's Ease and Sweet Basil seedlings. And some flamenco music, and the Chopin nocturnes she'd listened to with my father when they belonged to the Singapore classical music appreciation club.

My mother turned the music up louder in the weeks ahead. She didn't hear me ring her phone after work quite often, and I'd drive across the river panicking, to check she was okay.

※

One evening, she doesn't answer her door when I knock, and all her lights are off. I knock a long time, my heart slowly sinking, wondering if they've taken her away again to the mental health unit, or worse. Surely she wouldn't take her own life. Trembling, I take out my spare key to her door.

I open it to find her sitting in the light of a candle, listening to Spanish music.

'Sally Jones,' she says.

'Such beautiful music,' I reply.

'*Cante jondo*. Deep song.'

'Sounds like flamenco?'

'One of the flamenco family. A song sung originally by those living on the margins of society, expressing deep sadness and loss. One of the first kinds of flamenco singing.'

'Are you feeling very sad?' One of the few times I'd asked her that directly. She'd seemed sad so often, as far back into my childhood as I can remember. She lowers her eyes and doesn't answer me, but her mouth quivers. 'You sure you wouldn't like to come and stay with us a while, Mum?'

'Think it's best for me to stay here. I'll be alright.'

'Will you look after yourself?'

'Yes.'

'Promise?'

'Promise.' Her smile unfurling slowly, like the last line in the *cante jondo* unfurling through the speakers in her flat and out through the balcony door to her garden, where the willy-wagtails sing their evening song alongside it, transforming the *cante jondo* into something happier.

The candle flickers, showing her in yet another light. 'You look so beautiful. Can I take a photo?'

She inclines her head to one side, nods and smiles.

My university photography tutor had told me years before that photos taken with non-digital single lens reflex cameras can be blurred either by the vibration of the camera's mirror flipping up and down when the shutter is released, or by trembling in the photographer's breath and hands. If you're not using a flash in dim light, you can reduce the likelihood of blurring by resting your camera or your elbows on a stable surface and holding the camera firmly against your face. Then you breathe in, press the shutter button and stay very still, until the mirror drops down again.

But I can't steady myself enough when I take a photo of my mother that evening, thinking of how much further she had fallen while in the Mental Health Unit for Older Adults.

※

My mother's face by candlelight

Colour film. The candle beside her casts that side of her face and her silver hair a rich aged gold, the other side in shadow. But her eyes appear enormous, dark and astonished, because, of course, I've blurred her face. Just as well, I think when I see the print, for it'd be too painful to have a clear image of her that night, despite her beauty.

Reunion

DELAYING THE FINAL FREEZE

'THEY think he only has a few weeks to live,' my father's wife Trudi tells me on the phone, 'visit him while you can.'

✳

'How is ... your mother?' he asks.

'Okay,' I lie.

'Give her my love,' he says.

In the long silence that follows, Trudi bustles into his nursing home room, trim in her fitted jeans, jacket and boots.

'I was just about to leave,' I lie, kissing him on his forehead and backing into the corridor.

'I'll see you out,' Trudi says. She flicks her frosted fringe as we walk to the main entrance. 'I've started clearing his stuff out of the duplex. Got some in my car for you.'

She unlocks her shiny red hatchback, hands me a cardboard box. 'Throw this stuff away if you don't want it. Glad to get rid of it. Don't tell him.' How different from my mother Trudi is. I wonder if being a nurse has given her a lower tolerance for excess baggage and inefficiency.

✻

Only these mementos of my father's Singaporean life in the box with his discarded spectacles:

A small black and white post-war photo of his family.

The Rolex watch the Singaporean government had given him in acknowledgement of his work on the new pipelines, still ticking.

A shabby 1957 *Singapore Street Directory* with his small economical handwriting on several maps. A fading pencilled route my father might have followed in the early days of his working life, showing a journey between sewage tanks, reservoirs and other bodies of water, some of them marked by tiny faded X's. But larger X's mark Bukit Timah Hill, where he'd proposed to my mother all those decades before, and in the bottom right-hand corner of the map of Pasir Panjang overlooking the South China Sea, where they'd lived as newlyweds. Strangely, these larger X's are unfaded and written in the spidery writing of his old age.

The street names on the Pasir Panjang map are Malay, Chinese, Indian and English, suggesting a past and future full of promise. But so many of those roads led to nowhere on that map of my parents' early years together.

✻

'Would you like your old watch so you know the time?' I ask my father on my next visit, putting it on his bedside table. 'It's still working.'

'It'll ... work forever,' he says proudly. He looks out the window. 'When I courted your mother ... I had a photographer's ephemeris. But I lost it.'

'I'm sorry, Dad. It wasn't there amongst your things. But I brought your old Singapore street directory. Thought you could show me all the places that were important to you and Mum.' Sitting in his high-backed grey vinyl nursing home armchair, my father peers at the map of Bukit Timah where he'd written Home.

'Shh-ame Mercedes doesn't ... live there anymore. But the orchard mmight ... still be there. It was sss-o close to the reservoir they ... mmightn't have bulldozed it.' He looks sadly at me. 'I had a ... terrible time last night.'

'What kind of terrible time?'

'I couldn't eat any of that mmm-ush they're feeding me. Later I was ... arrested by the police for not ... having a passport. They locked me up to frrreeze to death in Singapore Cold Storage. I'm ... not ... sure ... how mmmuch ... lllonger ... I can ... go ... on.' I hear the long slow tremor in his voice, see it moving through his body. Repress my own shivering at his living nightmare.

I speak to the doctor in the corridor.

'The hallucinations are another symptom of the advanced stages of the disease. Maybe slightly aggravated by the new drugs we're giving him,' the doctor tells me.

My father complains when I return to his bedside.

'I was ... nursed yester ... day by a ... large woman with ... short blonde hair and ... a red face. She ... wouldn't to speak to me. Except to complain she can't ... understand my speech. She pushed ... mush into my mouth. Swore when I ... choked on it.'

I haven't met that nurse yet. I speak to the matron at the desk, but she says none of her nurses fit that description. Maybe the large nurse is one of my father's hallucinations, too. But I have no doubt he feels he is up against the great white wall again.

'I'm ... not ... sure ... how mmmuch ... lllonger ... I can ... go ... on,' he repeats. 'Sssorry ... the ... bbrroadcast's ... even more ... sslurred today,' he apologises. 'Like ... the BBC in ... Sssingapore when ... I was a child.'

Soon his illness will freeze him forever. It already demands all his willpower and concentration to swallow. He refuses the liquefied food offered by a nurse when the meal trolley comes.

'More tasteless ... mmush,' he complains. 'I ... will ... die f-aster ... if ... they mmake me ... eat ... that again. Ssspeech ... movement ... now even ... my food ... is ssslurred.'

His Rolex watch is smeared with puree and soup, but still keeping perfect time. How much longer will he live?

'Do you have anything tastier?' I ask the nurse.

'We don't cater for foreign appetites here,' the nurse tells me. 'The smell might distress the other residents. And there's duty of care. He's on a puree diet. He might choke on solid food.'

※

On my next visit, I bring him takeaway curry laksa, kuey teow and ginger tea, so that he might taste memories of Singapore. Anything to delay the final freeze. I feed him in his room, to avoid upsetting staff or residents.

'Thank…you.' His eyes close and he sighs with satisfaction. Two slow tears run down his face. 'Aunty… Mercedes…visited me…today.'

I don't have the heart to remind him that his sister Mercedes had died over three years ago in Singapore, and hadn't visited since I was a child.

'You know,' he says as he swallows the last of the food, 'I would like some photos of … where I came from. The family church. The orchard of my parents' home. Can you…go to Singapore and take them for me? And…bring me…some Jeyes disinfectant. The … disease is … everywhere.'

※

After the War

The small black and white post-war photo of my father's family. Dad, leaning forward on the threshold between late adolescence and early adulthood, wears chino trousers and a white short-sleeve shirt, his face boyish and eager for the life ahead of him. His sisters Mary and Mercedes, their smiles more restrained, wear full-skirted New Look dresses copied by their favourite tailor in Little India. They flank their seated parents.

Their father wears his harbour officer's trousers and white shirt. The war is still visible in his gaze.

Their mother wears a fine cotton kebaya-like jacket over a loose housedress, her goiter visible just above its neckline. Her gaze is as patient and suffering as a saint's.

Behind them all hangs a print of Christ revealing his fiery heart. They hung images of Christ in every room of their old British colonial bungalow, in gratitude for surviving the war.

But the mother and father are both gazing from this new life towards their death. Within two years of sitting for this photo, they will go to their graves not knowing that their son will meet his future first wife a whole ocean and many cultures away from them.

ENDLESSNESS

MY phone rang the next afternoon.

'Your dad's got pneumonia, love. He's falling in and out of consciousness,' said Trudi. 'Won't be long now.' She sounded almost relieved.

I still didn't know enough about my parents' early years together, but now the future episodes I'd been dreading rushed towards me.

I rang my mother as the seagulls circled above crying, as if farewelling something already lost.

'Dad's not very well. Want to visit him?'

'But I haven't seen him since the divorce.'

'He's dying, actually.'

'Pick me up straight away,' my mother said, sounding both more assertive and more shocked than I'd ever heard her.

※

She has put on her best summer dress. Age and years of avoiding the summer sun had lightened the hazel of her eyes and paleness of her skin. A few stray hairs wafted around her pale face in the warm breeze coming through the car window as we sped northwards up the freeway. As we passed the ornate brick facades and bleak backsides of faux-Tuscan and pseudo-Federation houses near the nursing home, she began crying.

'Maybe enough time has passed to wash away the secrets that got in the way of our marriage.'

'What secrets?'

'You're our daughter. It's not fair for me to burden you with them.'

'Mum. I'm an adult. I've already shouldered a few burdens.' We turned the corner and drove up the hill towards the nursing home.

'Maybe our stories will merge again. Ah, the ocean.'

※

My father's eyes are closed when we enter his room; his head sinking into his pillow. Have we arrived too late?

'Dad?' I say softly. 'I've brought Mum to see you.'

My father opens his eyes swiftly, reaches out his thin trembling hand to her and gazes at her face.

'My Love,' she says.

'Where've you been? I've been … waiting … years for … the dam to break,' he rasps. Mum sits in the vinyl chair, stroking his hand. 'How's the … garden?'

'Still growing. But in small pots now. Sorry to wake you.'

'I can't sleep … much. My … watch is … ticking … too loudly. Take it from the table,' he tells me. 'Sleep makes me … afraid. I was dreaming … I have no … passport and cannot … sstay.'

'Here or in Singapore?'

'The only … place I belong is in the … sewers. The underworld. With Hantu Maligang.'

'There is no new world without an underworld.' My mother sounds as if she's reciting. 'From the dream you had about Maligang when we were young. Remember?'

Dad closes his eyes. 'You remember his words from my dream … all … those years ago? You are a genius. And a saint too.'

My mother shakes her head. 'I have too many demons and ghosts to be a saint.'

'Maybe there are no … saints without demons?' he murmurs.

My mother turns to me. 'Give us some time alone together?'

I back through the doorway with his Rolex into the corridor, but can't stop myself from watching my parents. How many years have passed since I last saw them together?

'How are you feeling after that dream about not having a passport?' my mother asks him.

'I am tired … of longing. And of not … belonging.'

'Something else we have in common,' she says.

In the pause between them, I think about my father and his family when they were refugees during the war, eking out an existence in the Malayan jungle after the Japanese had banished them from Singapore. And I see that my mother is a refugee too, from that childhood trauma that haunts her, its ghost images now sometimes more real to her than the life she lives in plain sight of the present.

In the nursing home bed, my father's eyes widen with the effort of remembering and speaking. 'We never did ... find my ephemeris ... did we?'

'No, Love.' She pauses. 'We missed so many moments.' My mother taps her forehead with her forefinger. 'But here, our past remains present.'

My father closes his eyes. 'I could do with ... some longevity noodles from ... that hawker near the harbour in Singapore.'

She smiles. 'Ah. The ones we had on our wedding night.' She pauses a few moments, then speaks in a lower voice. In the corridor, I have to concentrate to hear what she's saying. 'I am sorry I wasn't very good in bed. I never told you something terrible happened to me when I was a small child, you see, which caused me pain when we ...' She glances up, sees me listening, stops talking.

I take a few steps back. The corridor is warm with the remains of that summer day, but I can't help shivering.

My mother murmurs something to my father that I can't hear.

'Why ... didn't you ... tell me ... all those ... years ... ago?' he rasps.

'I didn't know then what caused it. And I thought you wouldn't want me if I told you I thought there was ... something else wrong with me.'

Their murmuring stops. I peer through the doorway again. In the dim room, their gaunt old faces are only just visible. But I see that my father and my mother now understand each other more than they did when they were married. Through the window behind them, I think I can just make out waves rising and spending themselves on the shore, before returning and merging with the ocean.

'So much ... we haven't ... told each other,' my father finally says.

'How many of our stories stay untold because we're ashamed of them?' My mother pats the back of his hand.

'Shared history ... never ... ends ...' he replies. 'Even when ... two people are ... two different countries. Separated by ...'

In the long pause, I hear his watch ticking.

'Other bodies of water?' my mother smiles.

'The ocean of ... a lifetime,' he murmurs.

'Ah. Every body of water carries its stories, yes? Bringing its past into the present and future. Where they mingle with the stories of other watery bodies.'

He closes his eyes and smiles slightly, as if memorising her words. 'May ... be.'

'Our story shows that love, water, and time keep flowing between people like us. Despite our estrangement. And another thing,' she says more loudly as she catches sight of me through the doorway. 'We had a beautiful child, didn't we?'

My father nods proudly. 'And ... clever. Swam like ... a champion, even in your belly. Birth weight ... eleven pounds. What a ... monster.'

'The meeting of two civilisations. From which good things grow,' says my mother.

'How long ... will you ... stay ... with ... me?' he asks.

'How long do you want me to stay?'

'All the way to infinity lah,' he says, closing his eyes. And they fall silent as he floats through the twilight towards the darkest depths, but they grip each other's hands tightly, as if that might somehow stem the unstoppable flow of their lives away from each other.

※

Why did I write this? What really happened when my parents farewelled each other that evening?

When she walked with me into his room in the nursing home for the first and last time, she saw immediately he was too weak to do anything except listen to simple messages. So she kept to herself the story of being raped as an infant.

Instead, during that final twilight together, she told him how much she'd loved him, and still loved him, and would always love him. He said nothing, but squeezed her hand and looked directly into her eyes and nodded. In this way, they agreed on how enduring their love for each other had been. How unpredictably it had developed since my father's discussion with her about infinity decades before, when they'd first stood together on the shoreline of the Swan River as it wound towards the ocean of their futures.

My mother telling my father about her rape as an infant was just wishful thinking on my part. Because I thought it might have helped my father understand my mother better. Because I thought it might have helped explain to him why she'd been unable to become the kind of wife he'd wanted, despite all her efforts. Because maybe it would've helped the senseless rupture of their marriage finally make sense to them both.

❋

Only this

Their last twilight together. This image, unphoto-graphed, committed to memory only.

Her parchment-coloured hand, sunspotted, wrinkled, showing her old age more than his cinnamon-brown hand as they grip each other tightly, as if that might somehow stem the unstoppable flow of their lives away from each other.

Final Voyage

FINAL DIAGNOSIS

NOT long after my father dies, my mother tells me that she thinks her reflux problem is getting worse. She asks me to buy her Quick-Eze each time I ring to arrange a visit.

'It really helps to calm it all down,' she explains.

But after a few months, she tells me the Quick-Eze doesn't seem to be working any more.

※

Another new GP at her local clinic, a young woman she hadn't seen before, told her it was probably just worsening reflux, and prescribed her Nexium.

It seemed to work for a few more months, but then my mother told me she was having difficulty swallowing sometimes.

※

'Can you describe exactly how it feels?' the same young GP asks her. This time, I have insisted on accompanying my mother.

'Like the cookie monster on Sesame Street reaching up from my gullet,' she replies. The GP blinks behind her glasses, nonplussed.

'Mum. Be more precise,' I chide her. 'You told me when I picked you up it was painful this morning. Point to exactly where the pain is.'

She points to the base of her throat.

'We-e-ll,' says the GP, 'it may be an ulcer. I see on your records that you had a … stay in a … mental health facility. You can pick up stomach ulcers from staying in institutions.' My mother closes her eyes briefly. 'The least invasive procedure I can arrange for you to do is a breath test. But that won't necessarily be one hundred percent conclusive …'

'I would like something that's conclusive, and as soon as possible,' I cut in.

'An endoscopy then,' says the doctor, unnerved by my insistence, avoiding eye contact with me. She turns to my mother. 'That's when they put a tube with a little microscope down your oesophagus. But all the public clinics are booked out at least a few weeks in advance.'

'Oh please no,' my mother begs. 'I don't want a tube down my oesophagus. Nothing invasive.'

'Mum, I don't think we should waste time. I'll pay for a private specialist,' I tell the doctor.

'I've heard even the private ones are quite busy at the moment,' the doctor says.

'I don't care. Give me referrals to at least two, and I'll ring to get the earliest appointment,' I insist.

※

The birthday card she gives me later that week bears a photo of a hand pouring water from the tender pink interior of a large shell. The water falls into a sparkling sea that deepens near the horizon, into a blue so dark it's almost black.

'The same kind of shell we found on the South China Sea shore at Pasir Panjang when you were tiny,' she smiled. Inside she's written:

You've made so many voyages: of mind, of will, of heart, of the whole self, and I will never be able to thank you adequately for the many you've made towards me, often arduously. So I hope there are many more of a nurturing and delightful kind just along the track for you. All my love to you, who share so much and so beautifully: an outpouring.

That evening, I place the card in a folder, along with the others from her I've managed to keep over the years, despite my carelessness. Glancing through them, I see that her handwriting has always been meticulously formed, as if everything she writes is deeply considered. But it looks shaky and slants downwards in this last card, as if it's taken her much effort to keep going.

✳

'What do you want me to write under *Religion*?' I asked my mother as I filled out her admission form at the private hospital two weeks later. She'd tried various churches since divorcing my father, but not in the past few years. 'Christian?'

'No religion,' she said firmly. I wondered why she was so adamant about that, couldn't help hoping she'd found faith of another kind in herself. But I was interrupted by a nurse.

'It'll take a few hours, by the time she's come out of the anaesthetic,' the nurse said. 'Best for you to go back to work and we'll ring you.'

My mother looked even smaller and paler in the pale green hospital gown. I hugged her, stepped back and blew her kisses until the cubicle's blue curtain fell closed between us.

✳

My mobile phone rang much earlier than the nurse had suggested. It was the gastroenterologist who'd done the endoscopy. There was a slight tremor in his voice.

'I didn't have to go very far to find out the problem,' he said. 'I'm afraid there's a tumour in your mother's oesophagus. It started bleeding when I touched it with the tube. There's a high chance it's malignant, but they might be able to treat it. Buy her some time. I'm transferring her now by ambulance to

Charles Gairdner Hospital to get a full diagnosis and proper treatment. They're better equipped for this.'

I drove through the last heavy downpour of winter and ran unsheltered through the carpark to the emergency department of the hospital, the rain carrying my tears away as fast as they came. I felt I already knew the diagnosis: my mother's final death begins.

※

Inoperable and with a less than ten percent chance of chemotherapy working, radiation was the only treatment that might reduce the tumour and buy her time.

'We want to fatten her up a bit first,' the oncologist explained. 'Because it's too painful for her to swallow much food, we'll insert a stomach peg.'

※

My mother lay in another blue-curtained room with three other women. The nurses fed her magnesium and potassium intravenously; and high protein formula through her stomach peg.

She dreamed of lying with the other three patients swaddled in white cocoons, being fed milk through long teat-shaped tubes.

※

The radiographers showed us the tumour in the crosshairs on their screen. It made it all look so clean and precise, a winnable war.

But the effects on my mother were not clean, and her chances of winning were uncertain. The red stain growing on the pillowslip near her mouth every time I visited. Her face even paler than before, like a rose pressed too hard.

※

She asked me to do some banking for her, to bring from her kitchen counter her latest bank statement. There in the cramped public hospital room she shared with three other women, I discovered that she had set up regular payments from her bank account to at least half a dozen charities every month.

'Save the Children Fund, UNICEF, Médecins Sans Frontières, Aboriginal Medical Service, Red Cross. And here are more. Oh, Mum. Is this why you never had money left over from your pension at the end of every fortnight, even after you inherited that little sum from the sale of Nan and Grandpa's unit?'

She nodded, looked at me steadily. 'I'd like to keep those donations going for now.' Those waves of kindness in her which insisted on trying to carry others who struggled towards the shore, despite her fear of the terrifying depths beneath her.

※

The radiation treatment ran for six weeks. It brought up so much blood she had to stay in hospital for the duration, fed only on formula through the stomach peg and antibiotics through intravenous tubes.

'I miss my little flat,' she said.

'I'm keeping an eye on it. Your garden's still flourishing. I'll keep it alive.'

My inadequate substitute for guaranteeing the same for her life.

※

'She's in remission,' one of the treating oncologists said a few weeks later. 'She can return home. She can eat soft food.'

I didn't dare ask for how long. I held my mother's hand tightly. Then we packed her small suitcase with her nightdresses and drove back towards her flat.

In her suburb, she noticed residents putting out things for a verge clearance. We did a celebratory lap around the block, picking up a few wilting pot plants and an old calendar full of reproductions of European old masters' paintings from the Louvre. The pickings were more meagre than usual, but we were overflowing with relief about her remission. In the bookshop next to the café where she gratefully sipped a coffee, I bought her a calendar for the new year ahead.

※

But only weeks later, it became too painful for her to swallow even soft food.

The new scan showed little flames of bright colour in her lungs, kidneys and liver.

'Metastases,' said another oncologist apologetically. 'Time to start thinking about quality of life rather than quantity. We'll admit her again, try to get the pain under control.'

'So much for remission,' she said to me as we walked down the hospital corridors again.

※

The ward's night light shone in her eyes and gave her migraines. The nurses gave her painkillers and swapped her into a bed overlooking a small inner courtyard garden, dark and sunless, with only one ivy-like species covering the whole courtyard.

'But still a garden,' she said gratefully. There, she watched the days' and nights' light and darkness pass into a week.

When you are waiting for something that might make your short remaining life more bearable for an unpredictable time, what is the value of a day, what is the value of a night?

※

My mother is in the transitional-care nursing home, trying to learn how to feed herself through her stomach peg because food is still too difficult for her to swallow. On the way to visiting her, I buy a new mobile phone with a good camera in it. A camera with so many settings – wide-angle, zoom, panorama – all without changing the lens. I am like so many other photographers now.

✷

She can still swallow a good cup of coffee. I take her out every day for one at her favourite beachside café, while she waits in the nursing home to return to her flat. She is waiting for me now at the nursing home door.

'Sorry I'm late. I had to buy a new mobile phone. One with a good camera.'

'I thought you might not come,' she says. She wears her best straw hat and the summer linen dress I bought her from the opportunity shop the last time I'd taken her to Fremantle. I'd wanted to buy her some new clothes. No point in buying new clothes, she'd said. I'll be dead soon. The linen dress had never been worn, still had the tag attached and fit her perfectly. But as she'd sorted through the op shop's baskets of toys and artworks, I realised she was looking for some greater treasure. Signs of human tenderness? She'd been looking for those ever since I could remember.

'You look lovely,' I say as we drive to the beachside café.

'I love this dress. The colour of Singapore sunsets when the monsoon's over. And it's from the Save the Children Fund shop,' she smiles.

We pull up at the carpark next to the path that leads through the grass-silvered dunes. We glimpse the end of the path opening onto sunlight dancing on the opalescent ocean. When she leans on my arm as she gets out of the car, she feels almost weightless.

'One of my favourite trees,' she says, running her hand along the bronze-hued trunk of the coastal moort that shades the footpath leading to the Leighton Beach dunes. 'Your father and I planted one in the garden. Willy-wagtails nested in it, remember?'

'I heard them singing all night around full-moon time. Shall I take a photo of you under it?'

Through the viewfinder, she looks smaller and thinner than she's ever looked, yet her eyes still look achingly large and soulful, the way they had in all the photos of her my father had taken years before.

'I hope I don't look too – thin and sick.'

'You look beautiful.'

'A photo's just a memento of how a person looks at a particular moment,' she says, 'but a person's life floats across countless moments. We are all wandering in time, yet timeless. All the people I love. And when I close my eyes for the last time, I will still be seeing you all.'

I tap the shutter button once, twice, three times. How many photos of her will ever be enough?

'You're framed by the tree and the grassy dunes and backed by the ocean.' I lower the phone and give her my arm again.

'Ah, the Indian Ocean has often backed our little family, right?' She walks painstakingly slowly. Leaning on my arm, we take a long time to make our way past the dunes to the café. 'A person … must enter the wilderness,' she says as we walk. 'To find herself … and her own dreams. But some people … get lost and never return. Sorry I'm rambling,' she says. 'Just my cancer brain.'

Entering the café, we look up to see the afternoon sun backlighting and gilding a large square-rigged ship's sails as it cruises from Fremantle Harbour northwards towards the horizon.

'What is that? It looks like an old Portuguese sailing ship,' she says with awe.

'From the Age of Expansion?'

'Maybe. Or maybe it's come from beyond to carry me away to my … death.'

'I think it's the *Leeuwin* replica. It trains young people how to sail.'

'Ah, this world. This world and its people are so beautiful and life bewilders me still. And I am not ready to farewell them. I probably never will be.'

※

My mother wanted to return to her flat for as long as she could. In that month, she tended her little garden, planted some Heart's Ease seeds in an old saucepan, between the rosemary and lavender. I hoped she'd live long enough to enjoy their small purple and yellow faces smiling in the sun. But they didn't even germinate.

'Too late in the season,' she smiled sadly, 'too late.'

⁂

Another week-long stay in hospital. They insert a stent in her oesophagus so she might taste and swallow food again. It causes three days of terrible pain for her. On the fourth day, the pain from the stent subsides enough for her to swallow a soft meal.

'Bliss,' she says after her first hospital meal. Mash and poached fish, yoghurt for dessert.

'A white dinner in a white room.'

'Could do with a bit more colour. More important things to think about, though,' she said. She places her hand on her chest, brow furrowing.

⁂

That night after I leave, her heart falters badly. I don't hear about this until I visit her the next morning, and find she'd been moved in the middle of the night from the shared room to a single room.

'I made such a mess last night,' she tells me. 'Lost control of my body. Totally.'

'A side effect of severe atrial fibrillation. She came close to passing away,' a nurse says, reading the previous night's observation notes.

'Why didn't they ring me?' I ask.

'Didn't they?' The nurse looks alarmed. 'They should've.'

※

'Nothing more we can do for her. No point in her staying here any longer,' another nurse told me a day later. 'But there are no palliative care beds.'

'She can come and stay with me.'

'No. I don't want to risk imposing on you the terrible mess I made here the other night,' my mother insisted.

'I'd call an ambulance if that happened again, Mum.'

I spoke outside her room to the nurse.

'What if she has something like that heart fibrillation happen while she's with me? Will the ambulance come quickly enough?'

'I'll be honest,' said the nurse gently. 'Elderly woman with terminal cancer. She'd be last on the list if the ambulances are busy.'

※

That nurse finally secured my mother a palliative care bed in a hospital overlooking the river. I filled out my mother's admission form in her palliative care room, waiting, as instructed, for the ambulance to transfer her from the other hospital.

After completing the form, I watched the cumulus clouds of autumn slowly cover the sun above the river. Another hour passed. I rang Charles Gairdner Hospital but no-one knew where she was.

When she finally arrived, wheeled in by two ambulance officers on a stretcher, she was white, trembling and in pain.

'They left me in the corridor for hours. It seems I've waited forever to be rescued from beds in lonely places,' she murmured. That was all she said, as if she didn't have the strength to speak any more.

※

One lunch, one dinner. How many more might she eat? The three course meals at this hospital looked delicious compared to the previous hospital, and she carefully deliberated the choices on the next day's menu I read to her. But she could only swallow a little of each meal, so weak that I had to spoonfeed her. Yet she found the strength to open her arms to her now adult grand-daughter, in the way she had when she was a toddler.

My daughter begins sobbing.

'Don't worry,' my mother murmurs to her. 'I've had a good life.'

※

How long does she have? I was too afraid to ask.

'She could be here for weeks,' the palliative care doctor told me, as if he'd read my fear, 'maybe many. Or maybe she has only days.'

When you have such limited time remaining to live, what is the value of an hour, a minute, a second? What is the value of a smile?

※

Did she know then that she only had days to live? She told me one morning that when she closed her eyes, she saw the faces of the people she loved – some of them family, some of them friends, some of them almost strangers – carried in fast-moving, fluid currents.

'Like moving images from my life, illuminated.'

'Like a film?' I asked.

'*You* would say that,' she smiles, 'always a photographer. Always trying to capture moving bodies. I try to slow them down, so I can look at them for longer, remember them. But I can't, and then I realise there is no point in slowing them down. For how else will I get to see all the people and places I love before my life is over?'

※

'The painkillers don't work,' she murmured the next day. Hydro-morphine, sub-lingual bupra-morphine. 'There are too many different kinds of pain.'

※

The currents moving faster than any of us predicted. She gave up eating, yet seemed still to be waiting every day to see us.

She gave smiles, compliments, thanks in her soft voice to anyone in her room, right up to her last day.

A bouquet of basil, lemongrass, rosemary, eucalyptus leaves. Mother. I wish I'd thought to bring that to your final hospital bedside from the garden of memories you grew.

※

Her last moon floats boat-shaped above the river towards the Indian Ocean, shines through the window on her. She's light in my arms when I turn her to face the window, thinner and paler than I've ever seen her. Her voice, gentle as the night, vanished hours ago. All I can do is hold her hand and watch her slow retreat, like light from a body of water.

When her heart finally stops beating, I wish I'd taken one last photo of her before. Too late. It dawns on me as reluctantly as the grey autumn day outside, that she no longer dwells in her body. As her hand cools gradually in mine, I look in her nocturnal eyes and see I am utterly unprepared for all the days without her.

※

The last photo of my mother not taken

A close-up of her face, her dimming eyes showing her quiet strength and determination to keep giving to people, despite her pain and fear. And to endure uncomplainingly the grief of leaving this life, whatever it cost her, whatever lay on the other side.

After Images

LAST LIGHT

MY mother's lawyer writes to me after her funeral:

Your mother sometimes appeared fragile, but I believe she was an amazingly strong person. She was probably the closest I have come to a female version of Jesus. A living message from the beyond. She endured wrongdoing and violence from others but refused to pass any of that on. I believe she was a great woman and we were fortunate to know her.

I wonder how much he knows about her past. I think of asking him, but don't. For regardless of how much he knows, his appraisal of her seems true enough. Seen in a certain light.

I have not told all the stories I know about her, and there are doubtless others I will never know. What I know for sure: sometimes her depths were so dark she was unable to stop herself from passing the darkness on to those closest to her, but she regretted this deeply.

This memory of her telling my father the last time they saw each other, *I have too many demons and ghosts to be a saint.*

✳

Her stained old copy of Mrs Ellice Handy's *My Favourite Recipes* is coming apart at the spine on her flat's kitchen shelf. Inside it, I find one of my Eurasian grandmother's recipes, carefully handwritten by my mother. She's titled it *Rose's Subh Dehg (Blessed Pot)*.

Her turmeric gold fingerprint has faded in its margins. Translating my father's origins had been important to her. How carefully she'd tried to bridge his world and hers. With her cooking, her touch, her words; with her considered silence.

✳

During the months after my mother's death, I went a bit mad. Searched everywhere for messages from her. On scraps of paper in her books. In clouds coloured by the setting sun. In a small turban shell nestled beside a larger one on Port Beach's shore after that winter's first storm, the same kind of shell she'd shown me during my infancy on the Singaporean shoreline of the South China Sea. In music drifting through open windows at night. In the faces of strangers wandering the streets and shores of river and sea.

Looked, without realising it, for someone to love in the way I'd loved my mother.

Impossible.

※

Still my own voice wakes me from nightmares. I am shouting for my mother, for everyone who has been silenced by unspeakable violence. Shouting for our lives.

But in the broad light of days, I struggle to find words to tell the story. We who inherit familial trauma find it difficult to tell coherent stories about it, unfamiliar permutations of biography, fiction, nightmare, fragmented memory, erasure. Some of our attempts shine a light on long-hidden secrets, some conceal them further. Many of our attempts get stuck in our throats and pens, silenced by our fear of being judged. Perfect exposures are rare.

I dodge and burn, blur some details and change the names. To give me cover and courage for revealing these stories. My name is Sally Jones. My name is Eva Oliveira.

※

My mother had underlined two sentences in a book about wilderness photography I found open on the kitchen counter of her little palace of dreams: *Don't stop taking photographs too soon after the sun has gone down. It will continue to illuminate your landscapes long after it has disappeared below the horizon.*

Was this the last book she read? What kind of light did my nocturnal mother hold onto to help her face her blackest hours?

※

Mother of day and night, sun and moon. The golden light and the blue have passed into darkness. There is no ephemeris for charting death.

In that darkness, I've developed these images of her, some of them truer than others. Bearing in mind that just as a perfectly exposed photo is a manipulation of the truth, so is the story of a life. That every story we tell about someone else, is also a story about ourselves.

I have my demons and ghosts, as she did. But her courage in her life's darkest moments cast light for me then, and it lights my way still.

※

Even the coldest winter passes into warmer seasons. I put the two turban shells in my small front garden. They are empty, but the garden takes on new life. Children, friendships and my mother's plants grow, the seasons lengthen into another year.

The outer shells weather and darken, but their interiors are still the tender warm colours of a Singapore sunset when the monsoon has come to an end. I hold the large one to my ear. Listen for her voice. But there is only ocean.

ACKNOWLEDGEMENTS

This work of fiction is partly informed by my life and the lives of my parents. It also draws upon the following texts:

Singapore Street Directory and Guide, 1957: Survey Department, Government Publications Bureau, Singapore.

My Favourite Recipes, Ellice Handy, 1960: Malaya Publishing House Ltd, Singapore.

Singapore: An Illustrated History 1941–1984, VT Arasu and Daljit Singh (eds), 1984: Information Division, Ministry of Culture, Singapore.

Can Survive, La: Cottage Industries in High Rise Singapore, Margaret Sullivan, 1985: Graham Brash Ltd, Singapore.

From Dawn to Dusk, Ross Hoddinott and Mark Bauer, 2018: Ammonite Press – imprint of Guild of Master Craftsmen Publications, East Sussex, UK.

Popular Photography: The Complete Photo Manual, Marion Leuchter (ed.), 2012: Weldon Owen Inc., San Francisco.

100 Ideas That Changed Photography, Mary Warner Marien, 2012: Lauren King Publishing Ltd, London.

Some of the paragraphs about Francis as a young engineer in Singapore and as an old man in the nursing home are based on extracts from my short story 'The Asian Disease' in *Growing Up Asian in Australia,* Alice Pung (ed.), 2008: Black Inc., Melbourne.

'The Dark Room' contains a slightly different version of my short story 'Night Shifting,' published in *Westerly Magazine*, volume 64.1, 2019, Nedlands, Western Australia.

I am deeply grateful to the following people for their help while I wrote this book:

Associate Professor Susan Ash (Edith Cowan University, Perth) for insightful, generous feedback on several drafts of this book, and for years of encouragement and friendship.

Professor Isabel Carrera Suarez (University of Oviedo, Spain) – for offering me countless opportunities as a member of her research group, including space and time to revise this book, and to her and Robin Walker for boundless friendship and hospitality.

To my other incomparable friends Michael MacMahon, Tony Ayres, Linda Kwok, Sue and Greg Leaver, Maarten Renes and Fiona Fell for encouragement, hospitality and writing space during my revision and editing of this work in various cities in Australia and Spain. To other friends for helping me in many other ways during this book's writing, including Gloria Montero,

Lucy Dow, Rachel Horncastle, David Moody, John Lazarus, John and Raelene Troy. To Michael Cockram and his late wife Ronny, who helped my mother and me in many ways during difficult times; and for the phone text Michael sent me: my recollection of it directly informed the phone text in the section 'Last Light', though Michael's was more eloquent and longer.

Heartfelt thanks to my family: Anne, Mark and Catherine Lazaroo; Ken Rasmussen and my big-hearted, broad-minded offspring Sophia and Tom Rasmussen. And my late parents Judith and Ken Lazaroo, whose love and anecdotes have kept me going during the most difficult times.

Gratitude also to the wonderful team at Fremantle Press: Georgia Richter for her belief in my manuscript and for her superb editing, and to everyone else there whose hard work has enabled its journey into the wider world.

I acknowledge the Wadjak people of the Noongar nation as the traditional owners and custodians of Walyalup, where I live and work.

Finally, I acknowledge with thanks the Department of Local Government, Sport and Cultural Industries, for the grant enabling the writing of this book and Murdoch University for the honorary research fellowship.